THE BOY SCOUTS ON
STURGEON ISLAND

HERBERT CARTER

The Boy Scouts On Sturgeon Island

CHAPTER I

OUT FOR A ROYAL GOOD TIME

"Will you do me a favor, Bumpus?"

"Sure I will, Giraffe; what is it you want now?"

"Then tell me who that is talking to our scoutmaster, Dr. Philander Hobbs; because, you know, I've just come in after a scout ahead, and first thing saw was a stranger among the patrol boys."

"Oh! You mean that thin chap who came along in his buggy a bit ago, chasing after us all the way from that town where we had a bite of lunch? Why, I understand he's the son of the telegraph operator there. You know we made arrangements with him to try and get a message to us, if one came along."

"Whew! then I hope he ain't fetched a message that'll spoil all our fun, just when we've got to the last leg of the journey, with the boat only a few miles further on! That'd be the limit Bumpus. You don't know anything about it, I reckon?"

"Well, our scout-master looks kinder down in the mouth, and I'm afraid it must be some sort of a recall to duty for him," remarked a third lad, also wearing the khaki garments of a Boy Scout, as he joined the pair who were talking.

"I'm afraid you're right, Davy," said the tall, angular fellow who seemed to own the queer name of Giraffe, though his long neck plainly proved why it had been given to him by his mates. "But don't it beat the Dutch how many times Doc Hobbs has had to give up a jolly trip, and hurry back home, just when the fun was going to begin, because the old doctor he works with needed him the worst kind?"

"But say," spoke up the fat boy who answered to the designation of Bumpus, "mebbe the Cranford Troop, and the Silver Fox Patrol in particular, ain't lucky to have such a wide-awake, efficient assistant scout-master as our Thad Brewster, who knows more in a day about out-of-door things than Dr. Hobbs would in a year."

"Yes, that's right," replied Giraffe; "but we're going to know what's in the wind now, because here's the scout-master heading this way, with several of the other boys tagging at his heels, and sure as you live they're grinning too. Looks to me like Stephen and Allan thought it a good joke, though they look solemn enough when Doc turns their way. He's just got to leave us, you mark my words, fellows."

It turned out that very way. An urgent message had come that necessitated the immediate return of the scout-master. The old doctor with whom he practiced had been unlucky enough to fall, and break a leg; so it was absolutely essential that his assistant come back to look after the sick people of Cranford, hundreds of miles away.

While the scout-master is getting his personal belongings together, and the six boys gathered around are trying to look terribly disappointed, it might be well to introduce the little party to such of our readers who have not had the pleasure of making their acquaintance in previous volumes of this series.

The Cranford Troop of Boy Scouts now consisted of two full patrols, and a third was in process of forming. The original patrol was known as the Silver Fox, and the six scouts who were with Doctor Hobbs, away up here on the border of Lake Superior, bent on a cruise on the great fresh water sea, all belonged to that division of the troop, so that they are old friends to those who have perused any of the earlier books.

Thad Brewster, whom Bumpus had spoken of so highly, was a bright, energetic lad, who had always delighted in investigating things connected with outdoor life. He had belonged to a troop before organizing the one at Cranford, and was well qualified for being made the assistant scoutmaster, having received his credentials from the New York Headquarters long ago.

Allan Hollister, who would assume the responsibility should Thad be absent, was a boy who had spent quite a time in the Adirondacks before joining the scouts, and his knowledge was along practical lines.

Then there was another fellow, rather a melancholy chap, who had a queer way of showing the whites of his eyes, and looking scared, at the least opportunity, only to make his chums laugh; for he would immediately afterwards grin—in school as a little fellow he had insisted that his name of Stephen should be pronounced as though it consisted of two syllables; and from that day to this he had come to be known as Step Hen Bingham.

The other three boys were the ones who engaged in the little talk with which this story opens. Bumpus really had another name, though few people ever thought to call him by it; yet in the register at school he was marked down as Cornelius Jasper Hawtree; while the fellow who had that strange "rubber-neck" that he was so fond of stretching to its limit, was Conrad Stedman.

Davy Jones, too, wag a remarkable character, as may be made evident before the last word is said in this story. He seemed to be as nimble as they make boys; and was forever doing what he called "stunts," daring any of his

3

comrades to hang by their toes from the limb of a tree twenty feet from the ground; walking a tight-rope which he stretched across deep gully, and all sorts of other dangerous enterprises of that nature. Often he was called "Monkey," and no nick-name ever given by boy playmates fitted better than his.

Once Davy had been a victim to fits, and on this account gained great consideration from his teachers at school, as well as from his comrades. But latterly there had arisen a suspicion that these "fits" that doubled him up so suddenly always seemed to come just when there was some hard work to be done; and once the suspicion that Davy was shamming broke in upon the rest, they shamed him into declaring himself radically cured. It was either that, or take a ducking every time he felt one of those spells coming on; so Davy always declared the camp air had effected a miracle in his case, and that he owed a great deal to his having joined the scouts.

"Too bad, boys," said Dr. Hobbs, who was a mighty fine young man, and well liked by all the scouts in Cranford Troop, although they saw so little of him because his pressing duties called him away so often; "but I've got to go home on the first train. Doctor Green has a broken leg, and there's nobody to make the rounds among our sick people in Cranford. I never was more disappointed in my life, because we've fixed things for a glorious cruise up here on Old Superior."

The boys assured him that they deeply sympathized with him, because they knew it would break their hearts to be deprived of their outing, now that they had come so far.

"Fortunately," continued Dr. Hobbs, with a twinkle in his kindly eyes, "that isn't at all necessary; because all arrangements have been made, the boat is waiting only a few miles away, and you have an efficient assistant scout-master in this fine chap here, Thad Brewster, who will take charge while I'm away, as he has done on numerous other sad occasions."

"Hurrah!" burst from Bumpus; "that's the kind of stuff we like to hear. Not that we won't miss you, Doctor, because you know boys from the ground up, and we all feel like you're an older brother to us; but we've been out with Thad so much, we're kinder used to his ways."

"Well," continued the scout-master, with a long sigh, "I've got to hurry off if I expect to catch that afternoon train, and there's no other until morning; so good-bye, boys. Take good care of yourselves, and write to me as often as you can. I'll try and picture the jolly happenings of this Lake Superior cruise as I read your accounts of it."

He squeezed the hand of every one of the six lively lads; and there was a huskiness in his voice as he bade them a last good-bye that told better than words how sorry he was to leave the merry bunch, just when they were almost, as Bumpus put it, "in sight of the Promised Water."

So the vehicle passed from sight, and the last they saw of Doctor Hobbs was a hand waving his campaign hat to them just before a bend in the country road was reached.

All of them now turned to Thad to see what his plan of campaign would be.

"If it's just this way, fellows," he remarked, with one of his smiles that had made him the most popular boy in all Cranford, barring none; "we've got about three miles to hit it up before we reach the lake shore. Then we'll make camp and spend another night, which I hope will be our last ashore for some little time. Because, unless there's a hitch to the program, we ought to come on the landing where our boat is going to be in waiting, by ten o'clock to-morrow."

"Hurrah!" cried Bumpus, who was already weary of "hiking" because his build made him less active than some of the other scouts, notably Davy and Giraffe.

"Let's get a move on, then," suggested Step Hen. "I can see that poor old Giraffe here is nearly perishing for a little bite of supper."

A rippling laugh ran around at this, for every one knew the failing of the long-legged scout, whose stowage capacity when it came time to eat had never as yet within the memory of any comrade been fully tested; for they always declared that his legs must be hollow, for otherwise it was a mystery where all the food he devoured went to, since he never seemed to get any stouter after a meal than he was before.

The march was accordingly resumed, with Tad and Allan leading the van. The boys were going light, because they did not intend to do much camping on this trip, as it was expected that the boat would accommodate all of them with sleeping quarters.

Each one had a blanket strapped to his back, and with this were a few necessities in the line cooking utensils and food. Most of their luggage had been sent on by another route, as had also their supplies. Doctor Hobbs had wished them to go to the landing where their boat was to meet them, by following this roundabout course, having had some reason of his own for visiting the country. His folks in Cranford owned considerable land in this vicinity, and it was said that there were out-croppings of valuable copper to be found upon it; which accounted for the young man's desire to make inquiries while up in this region.

Joking and laughing, and even singing snatches of school songs, the boys of the Silver Fox Patrol tramped along the road that was to bring them to the shore of the lake by and by.

It was about half-past four when they obtained their first glimpse of the apparently boundless body of water, said to be the largest fresh water sea in the whole world. Shortly afterwards they reached the shore and were looking almost in awe out upon the vast expanse of water, upon the bosom of which they anticipated making their home for some weeks during vacation time.

"Here's the finest camp site you ever struck in your born days, fellers!" called out Giraffe, as he waved his arm around at the trees that grew close to the edge of the inland sea; and every one of the other five scouts agreed with him.

They had made many camps in the last two years, for they had wandered far from the home town, down in Tennessee, up in Maine, and away out to the Rockies on one memorable occasion; but no better place to spend a night had ever greeted their eyes.

It was soon a bustling scene, with a fire being started, and arrangements made to build a sort of lean-to shelter that would even shed rain in a pinch should a storm come upon them during the night they expected to spend here.

Davy, as usual, was climbing trees, and spying into every hole he could find. When Monkey Jones had a chance to exercise his peculiar gifts like this present opportunity afforded him it was utterly out of the question to hold him in. And so he swung daringly from one limb to another, just for all the world like a squirrel, chattering at times in a way that Giraffe always declared left no doubt in his mind concerning Davy's having descended from the original tree-climbing tribe that sported tails.

There was one very large tree close by, that is, large considering that in this section there were few that could boast a girth of more than a foot; but this one was really what Bumpus called a "whopper;" and Davy sported among the higher branches with all the delight of a child with a new toy; giving the others more than one thrill as he swooped this way and that with reckless abandon.

But suddenly he sent out a shout that caused every fellow to take notice; and Bumpus actually turned pale with apprehension, as he vainly looked around for some sort of weapon with which to defend himself; because he always believed he must be a shining mark for any hungry wild beast, on account of his plumpness.

"Oh!" shouted the boy in the tree, "a panther, fellers, a really true panther!"

CHAPTER II

THAD GOES AFTER THE YELLOW EYES

"He says a panther is up there!" echoed Giraffe, stretching that long neck of his at a fearful rate, in the endeavor to locate the animal in question.

All of them became immediately intensely interested in the further doings of Davy Jones. The boy chanced to be in a position where he could not apparently pass down the trunk of the tree, for fear lest he come in contact with the sharp claws of the dreaded beast which he claimed was hiding up there somewhere; but then that was a small matter to one so active as the Jones boy.

He immediately started to fearlessly slide down the outside of the tree, making use of the branches as he came along, to stay his program when it threatened to become too rapid.

The sight of Davy spinning down from that height with such perfect abandon, was one none of those fellows would ever forget.

When he finally landed on the ground they gathered around him with some misgivings, for Davy was addicted to practical jokes, and some of his chums suspected that even now he was, as Step Hen suggested, "putting up a job on his unsuspecting comrades."

One look at his really white face told them that at least Davy's fright had been genuine. He may not have seen a truly savage panther up there in the tree, but he firmly believed he did.

"Where was it, Davy?" demanded Giraffe, who had hastened to snatch up the camp hatchet in lieu of any better weapon with which to defend himself.

"Did it try to grab you?" asked Bumpus, with a tremor in his voice that he tried in vain to conceal by a great show of assumed bluster.

"And was there only one up there?" queried Step Hen, anxiously, fingering the double-barreled Marlin shotgun, which was the only firearm they had with them, as this expedition had not been organized with any idea of hunting; and the season for game was not on as yet, either, even in this northern country; though Giraffe, who owned the gun, had fetched it in the hope that they might be forgiven if they knocked over a few wild ducks, should their rations run low.

"I didn't wait to ask," stammered Davy, "fact is, boys, I didn't really see the terrible beast at all, only his big yellow eyes!"

"Oh! is that so, Davy?" exclaimed Thad, turning to give Allan a wink, as much as to let him understand that the truth would soon be coming now.

"But see here," Step Hen wanted to know; "however was you agoin' to see his eyes and not glimpse the panther himself; that's a thing you've got to explain, Davy Jones."

The other bent a look of commiseration on the speaker.

"What's the answer to that?" he went on to say, recovering his voice more and more with each passing second, now that his personal safety seemed assured; "I'll tell you, Step Hen. You see, there's a big yawning gap in the tree up there, as black inside as your hat after night. And when I just happened to look that way what did I see but a pair of round yellow eyes astaring straight at me! Guess I've seen a panther, and I ought to know how his eyes look in the dark—just like you've seen the old cat alooking at you to home, when you went into a dark room. Wow! say, did you notice me acoming down that tree outside like greased lightning? I own up I expected I'd be pounced on any second, and that made me in something like a hurry, fellows!"

One or two of the scouts snickered at this. The sound appeared to annoy

Davy, who was plainly very much in earnest.

"Huh! easy to laugh, you fellows," he remark, with deep satire in his voice. "Mebbe, now, you, don't believe what I'm telling you! Mebbe one of you'd like to just climb up there, and see for yourself what it is? I dare you, Bumpus!"

"You'll have to excuse me, Davy; it's too big a job for a boy built like me, you understand, though sure I'd like to accommodate first rate," replied the scout with the red hair and mild blue eyes, shrinking back, and shrugging his shoulders.

"Then how about you, Step Hen," pursued Davy, determined to put it to each of the scoffers in turn until he had shown them up in good style; "I notice that you're looking like you didn't reckon there couldn't abeen such a thing as a genuine panther around this region in the last twenty years and more. Suppose you tumble up there, and take a look-in!"

But the party indicated smiled sweetly, and laid his hand on the region of his stomach, as he went on to say:

"Why, really and truly, Davy, I think I'm going to have one of those nasty cramps just like you used to have so often. There's agripe coming on right now, and you see how unpleasant it would be to find myself doubled-up while I was thirty feet from the ground. I'm afraid I'll have to pass this time."

"Then, there's Giraffe who'll he sure to volunteer," continued the other, bound to take all the scoffers in by turns. "He's of an investigating turn of mind, and if he wants to, I reckon he might take that gun along, so he could have some show, if the thing jumped right out in his face!"

"Well, now," the long-legged scout answered, with a whimsical grin, "I'd like to accommodate you the worst kind, Davy, but you know how it is with me. I ain't worth a cooky before I've had my feed. Feel sorter weak about the knees, to tell you the honest truth; and I never was as keen about climbing to the top of tall trees as you were, Davy. Count me out, please, that's a good fellow."

At that Davy laughed outright.

"I see you've got cold feet in the bargain, Giraffe," he asserted. "Well, then, if anybody's going to climb up there and poke that ugly old beast out of his den it'll have to be either our scout-master, or Allen; for I tell you right now you don't catch me monkeying with a buzz-saw after I've had my fingers zipped."

"I'll go," said Thad, quietly.

"Here, take this, Thad," urged Step Hen, trying to force the shotgun into the hands of the other, as he stepped toward the base of the big tree.

Thad and Allan again exchanged looks.

"Don't think I'll need it, do you, Allan?" the former asked.

"Hardly," came the reply; "and even if you did carry it up, the chances are you couldn't find a way to hold on, and shoot at the same time. Here, let me take that thing, Step Hen; you're that nervous. If anything did happen to fluster you, I honestly believe you'd up and bang away, and perhaps fill our chum with bird-shot in the bargain."

Step Hen disavowed any such weakness, but nevertheless he was apparently glad to hand over the weapon; because he realized that Allan knew much better how to use firearms than he did, and if there was any occasion for shooting, the responsibility would be off his shoulders; for Step Hen never liked to find himself placed where he was in the limelight and had to make good, or be disgraced.

Thad did not appear to be at all worried, as he took a last good look aloft, as though wishing to assure himself that there was no panther in sight among the thick branches above, before he trusted himself up there.

His good common sense told him that the chances were as ten to one that Davy had not seen what he claimed at all; but his fears had worked overtime, and simply magnified some trifling thing.

9

Of course had Thad really believed there was any chance of meeting such a savage beast as a panther he would never have ventured w make that climb; or if he did he must have surely taken the gun along with him.

The others gathered around near the foot of the tree, and tried to follow the daring climber with their eyes, meanwhile exchanging more or less humorous remarks in connection with his mission.

All of them, saving possibly Allan, seemed to be a little nervous concerning the outcome; because Davy kept on asserting his positive belief that it was a real true panther that lay in the aperture above, and not a make-believe.

"I only hope Thad can dodge right smart if the old thing does come whooping out at him!" was the way Davy put it; at which the eyes of Bumpus grew rounder and rounder, and he began to quietly edge away from under the tree, an inch at a time; for he hoped none of his chums would notice his timidity, because Bumpus was proud of having done certain things in the line of bagging big game, on the occasion of their trip to the Far West.

"There," remarked Step Hen, "he's getting up pretty far now, and I reckon must be close by the place where you saw your old panther, Davy."

"Yes," added Giraffe, "and you notice that Thad's marking time, so to speak, for he's hanging out there, and trying to see what's above him."

"A scout should always use a certain amount of caution," interposed Allan; "there are times when a fellow might take chances, if it's a case of necessity, and quick action is necessary in order to save life; but right now Thad's only carrying out the rule he's always laid down for the rest of us.

"Be prepared, you know, is the slogan of every scout, and that's what he's doing. He wants to be sure of his ground before he jumps."

"Hub!" grunted Davy, "if I'd stopped to count ten before I slid down, I wonder now what would have happened to me. Some fellers act from impulse every time, and you can't change the spots of the leopard, they say. What's dyed in the wool can't be washed out, as took as Bumpus here with his carroty hair."

"You leave my hair alone, Davy Jones, and pay attention to your own business," complained the stout scout, aggressively. "You just know you're a going to get it when Thad makes his report, and you're trying to draw attention somewhere else. Make me think of what I read about the pearl divers when they see an old hungry man-eating shark waiting above 'em; they stir up the sand with the sharp-pointed stick they carry; and when the water gets foggy they swim away without the fish being able to see 'em. And you're atrying right now to befog the real case, which is, did you really see anything, or get scared at your own shadow."

"Hear! Hear!" crowed Giraffe, who always liked to see Bumpus aroused, and when this occurred he often made out to back him up with approval, just as some boys would sick one dog on another, or tempt rival roosters to come to a "scrap."

"You fellow's let up, and watch what Thad's agoin' to do," Step Hen advised them at that juncture; and so for the time being Davy and Bumpus forgot their complaint and riveted their eyes on the boy who was up in the tree.

"I can't hardly see him any more, the branches are so thick," complained

Bumpus ducking his head this way and that.

"That's because he's gone on again," argued Giraffe; "seems like he didn't find any signs of a real panther when he took that survey."

"Hold your horses!" was all Davy allowed himself to say, though no doubt he himself had commenced to have serious doubts by now.

Half a minute later and there broke out a series of strange sounds from up above their heads.

"Listen to that, now, would you?" cried Davy, bristling with importance again. "Don't that sound like Thad might a hit up against something big? Hear him talking, will you? Didn't you catch what he said right then—no, you don't grab me, you rascal; I'm afraid I'll have to knock you on the head yet! Say, don't that sound like Thad had found my panther, and was keeping him off with that club he took up with him. Oh! what's that?"

Something came crashing down as Davy uttered this last exclamation. The boys were horrified at, first, because they imagined it might bit Thad and the panther, that, meeting in midair, had lost their grip, and were falling to the ground, fully forty feet below.

"Why, it's only his club," cried Giraffe, quickly.

"Then he must have let it get knocked out of his hand!" ejaculated Bumpus. "Oh! poor Thad. He'll be in a bad fix without a single thing to fight that animal with!"

"That's where you're mistaken, because I can see him now, and he's acoming down the tree right smart!" Step Hen announced; which intelligence allowed Bumpus to breathe freely again, for his face was getting fiery red with the suspense that had gripped him.

11

"That's so!" echoed Giraffe, "and I'm looking to see if there's any signs of a big cat trailing after him, but so far nothing ain't come in sight."

The five scouts on the ground hastened to close in around the foot of the big tree, so as to welcome their patrol leader when he dropped from the lower limb.

"Seems to me Thad acts kind of clumsy, for him," announced Step Hen; "now, if it'd been Bumpus here I could understand it, because, well I won't say what I was agoing to, because it might make hard feelings between us; and with all his shortcomings Bumpus is a good sort of a chap."

"Huh! dassent, that's what!" grunted the party indicated, making a threatening gesture in the direction of his fellow-scout.

The arrival of the scout-master caused them to forget all other things. Thad, as soon as he found his feet fixed on solid ground once more, strode straight up until he faced Davy Jones, and suddenly called out:

"There's your panther, Davy!"

There was a craning of necks, a gasping of breaths, and then a series of yells broke forth that made the nearby woods fairly ring with the echoes.

CHAPTER III

THE CAMP ON THE LAKE SHORE

"Why, it's only a big owl!" shouted Giraffe.

"Hey, Davy, shake hands with your yellow-eyed panther!" roared Step Hen.

Bumpus snatched up his bugle, for he held that office in the Cranford Troop, and let out a piercing series of blasts that would have undoubtedly frightened any wild animal, had there been such within a mile of the camp on the lake shore.

It was a large owl that Thad grasped in such fashion that the bird could not reach him with its curved beak, though it made several vicious lunges, as though anxious to fight the whole patrol at once.

He had kept it hidden under his coat when descending the tree, and now gripped it firmly by its two splendidly colored wings.

"Well, it did have yellow eyes, all right," complained the dejected Davy; "and as it stuck there in that black hole, how was I to know it was only a harmless old owl, a hooter at that?"

"If you think he's harmless just try and lay a finger on him," said Thad. "Why, he'd snap you like lightning; once let that beak strike, and you'd lose a piece of skin as big as a half dollar. He's a savage bird, let me warn you."

"Oh! say, can't we, keep him for a pet?" ejaculated Bumpus, who could hardly take his eyes off the bird, for its plumage was certainly beautiful, being a combination of creamy yellows and nut browns, while two bunches stuck up like horns from the region of his ears.

"I've got a nice little chain we might put around one of his legs, and what fun we'd have with the thing while we were afloat on the raging lake," Step Hen went on to say.

"Allan, get on that thick pair of gloves we brought, and see if you could fasten the chain to his leg. It would be worth while to have some sort of pet along with us; because Bumpus has kicked over the traces long ago, and won't let us make a baby out of him any more," Thad went on to remark.

When he had protected his hands in this way, Allan had little difficulty in adjusting the slender but strong steel chain which Step Hen had brought with him, intending to use in case he managed to capture a raccoon, or some other small beast, for he was especially found of pets.

When they had fastened the other end of the chain to something, the owl sat on the limb of a tree, and gazed at them with blinking eyes. There was still

13

enough of daylight, with all that glow in the western heavens to interfere with his sight more or less, and he simply ruffled up his feathers in high dudgeon, and kept trying to pick at the chain that held his leg.

"Now, that's what I call a pretty good start," argued Step Hen, as he stood in front of the chained owl, and admired his plumage; "perhaps later on I might happen to land a 'coon or a mink, who knows. I've always believed that I'd like to have a pet mink, though somebody told me they couldn't be tamed."

"Yes," went on Giraffe scornfully, "if you had your way the whole boat'd be a floating menagerie, you've got such a liking for pets. The mink would soon be joined by a 'possum; then would come a pair of muskrats; after which we'd expect to find a fox under our feet every time we stepped; a wolverine growling like fun at us when we made the least move; a squirrel climbing all over us; a heron perched on the garboard streak, whatever that might be; and mebbe a baby bear rolling on the deck. All them things are possible, once Step Hen gets started on his collecting stunt."

"Well, forget it now, won't you, Giraffe, because there goes Bumpus putting supper on the fire; and unless you look sharp he'll just cut down your ration till you'll only get as much as any two of us," advised Step Hen.

In spite of all these little encounters of wit, and the sharp things that were sometimes said, boy fashion, these six churns were as fond of each other as any lads could possibly be. There was hardly anything they would not have done for one another, given the opportunity; and this had been proved many times in the past.

While they were fond of joking the tall scout on his appetite, truth to tell every one of the others could display a pretty good stowage capacity when it came to disposing of the meals. And so they were all anxious to help Bumpus when he started getting the camp supper ready.

Besides these six lads there were of course two others who went to, make up the full complement; of the Silver Fox Patrol; and who have figured in previous stories of this series.

These boys were named Robert Quail White, who was Southern born, and went by the name of "Bob White," among his friends; and Edmund Maurice Travers Smith, conveniently shortened to plain "Smithy."

These two had taken a different route to the lake, and expected to meet their six churns at a given rendezvous. They were intending also to make use of another boat, since the one engaged for the party would only accommodate seven at a pinch, and counting the scout-master they would have numbered nine individuals in all.

The other two had found that they wanted to see the wonderful Soo Canal, and the rapids that the St. Mary river boasts at that point, where the pent-up waters of Superior rush through the St. Mary's river to help swell the other Great Lakes, and eventually pass through the St. Lawrence river to the sea.

It is no joke cooking for half a dozen hungry scouts, and the one whose duty compelled him to be the chef for a day had to count on filling the capacity of coffee-pot and frying-pans, of which latter there were two.

Evening had settled down upon them by the time they were ready to enjoy the supper of Boston baked beans, fried onions with the steak that had been procured at the last town they had passed through; crackers, some bread that one of them toasted to a beautiful brown color alongside the fire, and almost scorched his face in the bargain; and the whole flanked by the coffee which was "like ambrosia," their absent chum Smithy would have said, until they dashed some of the contents of the evaporated cream into each tin cup, along with lumps of sugar.

"This is what I call living," sighed Giraffe, as he craned his neck visibly in the endeavor to see, whether there was a third "helping" left in the pan for "manners," which was another name for Conrad Stedman.

"Hadn't we better save this piece of steak for Tim?" suggested Step Hen, wickedly, for that was the name he had given to the captive owl.

"No, you don't," objected Giraffe, vociferously, just as the other had known he would do; "that's the very last beef steak we're apt to see for half a moon; and I say it would be a shame to waste it on a heathen bird. Besides, you couldn't coax Jim to take a bite till he's nearly starved; ain't that so, Thad?"

They always appealed to either the assistant scout-master or Allan, whenever any question like this came up, connected with bird or animal lore; and no matter how puzzling the matter might seem to the one who asked, it was promptly answered in nearly every instance.

"Yes, he isn't likely to take hold for a day or two," replied Thad. "By that time the old fellow will sort of get used to seeing us about; and he won't refuse to eat when you put something out for him; only all of you be careful that he doesn't prefer a piece out of your hand. Don't trust him ever!"

"You can make up your mind I won't give him a chance to grab me," asserted Bumpus, never dreaming that by accident he would be the very first to feel the force of that curved beak.

"Listen!" exclaimed Step Hen; "as sure as anything there's another!

Why, this must be what you might call Owl-land."

15

From far away in the timber came the plain sound of hooting. All of the scouts knew what it was easily enough, though there had been a time when they were real tenderfeet, and could hardly distinguish between the call of an owl and the braying of a donkey; but camping-out experience had done away with all such ignorance as that.

"There, don't that make you feel foolish, Step Hen?" demanded Bumpus.

"Me? Whatever put that silly notion into your head, Bumpus?"

"Why," the other went on to say reproachfully, "it was you that really wanted to keep the poor old bird; and just listen to its mate mourning for it, would you? I'd think you'd feel so sorry you'd want to unfasten that chain right away, and give the owl its freedom."

"Not for Joseph, though I'll let you go and undo his chain if you feel inclined that way," Step Hen observed, knowing full well that Bumpus did not want to see the feathered captive set free quite that bad. "Besides, how d'ye know that's a mate to my bird whooping it up back there?"

"Well, if you want to find out, just you sleep with one eye open," Bumpus told him; "and take it from me you'll see that other owl come winnowing around here, wanting to know why our new pet don't come when she calls."

"Huh! mebbe I will,"' was all Step Hen would say about it; but evidently the idea had appealed to him; and there was a chance that he would indulge in very little rest that night, for trying to "keep one eye open while he slept."

After supper was all over, and the boys lay around on their blankets, they fell to talking of other days when they had been in company, and met with a great many, surprising adventures.

Then Bumpus, who really had a very fine tenor voice, which he could strain so as to sing soprano like a bird, was coaxed to favor them with a number of selections, the others coming in heavy in each chorus.

Sometimes it was a popular ballad of the day that Bumpus gave them; but more often a school chorus, or it might be some tender Scotch song like "Comin' Through the Rye," "Annie Laurie," or "Twickenham Ferry;" for boys can appreciate such sentiments more than most folks believe; and especially when in an open air camp, with the breeze sighing through the trees around them, or the waves murmuring as they wash the sandy shore of a lake, and the moonlight throwing a magical spell upon all their surroundings; for there is the seed of romance in the heart of nearly every healthy lad.

So the evening wore on until some of them began to yawn frequently, showing that they were ready to turn in. As one of them had said, this might be the last time they would camp ashore during trip, because on the morrow

16

they anticipated, unless something unforeseen came up to prevent it, going aboard their boat, and starting on the cruise upon the big waters of Superior.

They had no tent on this occasion, but really that was not going to prove any hardship to these bold lads, accustomed to spending many a night in the woods, with only a blanket for a cover against the dew and frost.

It was arranged to keep the fire going. This would serve in a double capacity, for not only would they be kept warm through the cold part of the night, but if there did happen to be any wild beasts around in that section of the Lake Superior country, which both Allan and Thad rather doubted, why, the glow of the blaze was apt to make them keep their distance.

The last thing Giraffe remembered, as his heavy eyes persisted in closing, was seeing Step Hen bob up his head to stare over toward the low branch upon which the captive owl was fastened; as though he might have arranged a program with himself and meant to do this thing at stated intervals all through the night.

Giraffe chuckled at the idea of sacrificing good sleep in the interest of knowledge; he was willing to simply ask some one who knew, and be satisfied to accept their answer as conclusive.

An hour later and the camp seemed to be all quiet, for every one was apparently sound asleep. Even Thad and Allan had known of no reason why a watch should be maintained, for they felt sure there could hardly be a human being within miles of the camp; and even if this were not so, the chances were strongly in favor of its proving to be an honest farmer, or some miner on his way to the workings further west.

The only sounds that could have been heard from time to time were an occasional peevish fretful croak from the captive owl, as it continued to peck savagely at the chain around its leg; or it might be a snore from Bumpus, or some other fellow who had a fashion of lying squarely on his back.

Perhaps pretty soon, when one of the scouts had been kept awake by this noise until patience ceased to be a virtue, he would get quietly up, and pour a tin-cup of lake water over the one who persisted in sleeping with his mouth wide open; for that sort of radical remedy had proven effective on other occasions, and brought relief.

It must have been almost midnight when a sudden change came about that took even the seasoned campers by surprise, for they had not been anticipating any such startling event.

The stillness was broken by a piercing scream that caused every head to bob up, and the blankets to be hurriedly thrown aside.

"My owl's mate has come in on us, mebbe!" exclaimed Step Hen; for that idea was so firmly lodged in his brain that it had to occur to him as soon as he heard all that row.

But some of the others were wiser, for they knew that shout had surely come from human lips.

Giraffe was the first to call out and draw their attention to certain facts.

"Looky there at old Bumpus dancing a jig, will you! Whatever ails the feller, d'ye think! Acts like he'd clean gone out of his head, and got loony!" he cried, as with the other boys he came tumbling out from under the rude shelter made of branches.

CHAPTER IV

LAUNCHED ON THE INLAND SEA

Sure enough Bumpus was in plain sight, for the fire still burned, and there was also a bright moon high up in the heavens. The fat scout seemed to be trying to execute all the steps in a Southern hoedown, or an Irish jig; for he was prancing around this way and that, holding on to his hand, which the other boys now discovered was streaked with blood!

"Oh! what's happened to you, Bumpus?" cried Step Hen, as he ran out toward the spot where the other continued to waltz around in his bright red and white striped pajamas, that made him look like an "animated sawed-off barber's pole," as one of his chums had once told him.

"It bit me, oh! I'll bleed to death, I reckon now!" wailed the other; "say, Thad, get out some of that purple stuff you use for scratches from wild animals. Mebbe blood, poisoning'll develop; and I'd just hate the worst kind to die up here, away off from my own home."

"What bit you; can't you tell us, Bumpus?" asked Thad, though already he may have had suspicions that way.

"Jim did, the bally old owl!" came the dismal answer; "please, oh! please tell me whether his beak is poisonous, won't you, Thad?"

"Well, what d'ye think of that?" ejaculated Step Hen, "however did you happen to meddle with my owl, tell me? Sure, I did give you permission to unchain him, if you had the nerve; but I never did believe you'd go and take me up at that."

"I didn't neither," Bumpus declared, still dancing around.

"Here, let me see that wound!" called out Thad, as he and Allan cornered the sufferer; "all it may need is washing, and then binding up with some healing salve. But it makes a nasty cut, don't it, Allan?"

"I should say yes," replied the other; "but it's some lucky it wasn't his face the bird struck at. Why, Bumpus might have lost an eye."

At that possibility the fat scout set up another roar.

"Just you believe the old thing meant to snap my eye out when he bit at me; and I must have happened to put out my hand—so he struck that!" he declared; while Allan hastened to open a package and take out some salve and tape such as scouts should always carry along with them when in camp, because there is no telling when it may be needed badly, just as in the present instance.

"But see here, what possessed you to walk around in this way, and go over to try and pet that savage bird?" asked Thad.

"Give you my solemn affidavit that I don't know a single thing about it!" the other went on to say, as solemn as the owl that sat on the branch near by.

"Do you mean you don't remember getting up, and coming out here?" continued the scout-master, who always probed things to the very dregs, or until he had extracted all the information possible.

"Not a thing," reaffirmed Bumpus, and his face showed that he was speaking only the truth. "I can remember laying down for a snooze, and then everything seems to be blank after that, till all of a sudden I felt that awful pain, and it made me let out a whoop, I'm telling you."

"I should think it did," muttered Giraffe; "ten Injuns rolled into one couldn't beat that howl. I sure thought the panther had got you that time!"

"Well, likely I thought just that same thing, Giraffe, when I warbled that way, because I remember now I was dreaming about gray-coated panthers. Then I thought about rattlesnakes too, because you know I can't stand for the crawlers. Next thing I opened my eyes with a jump, and saw that old owl, with every feather on his back standing up like the quills of a porcupine, and trying to jab me a second time."

Thad and Allan, who had now returned in time to hear this last exchanged looks.

"A clear case of sleep walking, seems like!" ventured the former.

"Oh! my goodness gracious! I thought I was over them tricks years ago!" exclaimed Bumpus, shivering. "If they're agoing to take me again I see my finish; because some night I'll walk off a precipice, and that'll be the end of me."

"We'll like as not have to tie you by the leg every night, just like Jim is now; and that'll stop you prancing around loose, trying to set my pets free in your sleep," Step Hen went on to say, reassuringly; but somehow Bumpus did not seem to take to the idea the least bit.

"You let me alone, that's all, Step Hen Bingham," he told the other, "and I'll fix my own business. That's what comes of you keeping the silly old owl. Serve you about right if his mate dropped in and bit the end of your big toe off to pay you up for fastening that chain on the poor thing's leg."

"Say, I like that, now; when you were the very first one to ask if we couldn't keep that same owl!" Step Hen told him.

"Wow! that hurts some, let me tell you, fellows!" groaned the fat scout, when Allan was putting some salve, calculated to help heal the wound, on the torn place, and then with the assistance of the scout-master started binding the hand up with windings of soft linen that came in a tape roll two inches wide.

"But let me tell you it's some chilly out here, with only pajamas on," objected Giraffe; "and for one I'm going to skip back under my blanket, where I can snuggle down. Somebody remember to throw a little wood on the fire, please. Let Davy do it."

Of course that really meant either the scoutmaster or Allan; and Giraffe often had a failing for shirking some duty like this. It was so easy to expect some other to do disagreeable things; though as a rule the boys were accustomed to saying, "let Davy do it," until it had become so tiresome that the Jones boy had rebelled, and refused to be the errand boy any longer for the entire patrol.

In half ah hour silence again brooded over the camp. Bumpus must have done something to make sure he did not start walking in his sleep again, for nothing occurred to disturb their slumbers until dawn came along and, with birds singing, as well as gray squirrels barking lustily at the intruders, awakened them all.

Breakfast was hurried, because all of them were' anxious to be on the move. They knew that by following the shore of the big water several miles they would come to the point where there was a village, with something of a landing place in a sheltered nook; and here they expected to find their boat awaiting them.

It was about an hour after sun-up that the cheery notes of Bumpus' silver-toned bugle gave the signal for the start; and the six khaki-clad lads could be seen moving at a fairly fast pace along the shore of the lake. Step Hen had managed to bundle the captive owl in a spare sweater, so he could carry him all right without danger.

The little waves came purling up close to their feet, and seemed to welcome the strangers to their domain; but Thad knew full well that under different conditions these same waves would unite to threaten them with destruction.

Step Hen having found a way to muzzle the owl, so that he could carry the prisoner, without fear of dire attacks from that sharp beak seemed more determined than ever to try and keep Jim; and he frowned every time he saw Bumpus observing the bird thoughtfully, because he imagined the fat scout might be hatching up a scheme for choking the thick-necked prisoner, in revenge for what he had suffered from its savage thrust.

Finally a loud shout was heard from Giraffe, who, being so much taller than the balance of the scouts, and possessed of a neck he could stretch to an alarming degree, was in a position to see much further than the rest.

"The village is in sight!" he announced, whereat there was a cheer, the owl commenced to struggle afresh, and Step Hen had his hands full trying to quiet his feathered prisoner.

With their goal now close at hand the boys were able to step out at a more lively pace, even Bumpus showing surprising gains.

About ten o'clock they arrived at the settlement where they had seen some sort of dock, at which a couple of ore barges of the whaleback type were being loaded.

Already the eager eyes of the boys had discovered a boat that answered the description of the one they expected to find awaiting them.

Making straight for the place they found that they had guessed rightly. That good sized powerboat was the Chippeway Belle, the vessel which was to be their home for the next two weeks or more, as they pleased.

An investigation revealed the fact that their stores were all aboard, as well as their extra supplies that went under the general designation of "duffel."

"Nothing else for us to do but go aboard, and make a bully start, is there, Thad?" asked the impatient Giraffe, eager to find out how the craft could go; for up to now the Silver Fox Patrol had generally spent their outings on dry land; and this idea of a cruise had come somewhat in the shape of what Thad called an "innovation."

"Nothing at all, Giraffe," replied the other, himself looking pleased at the prospect of being about to start on such a splendid pleasure trip.

"How about paying for the use of the boat; has all that been attended to?" asked careful Bumpus, who was not so very much of a water-dog himself, and rather viewed the prospect of getting out of sight of land on board so small a craft with anything but exultant delight; indeed, to tell the honest truth, the fat scout was already secretly sorry he had come.

"Oh! yes," replied Thad, quickly; "Dr. Hobbs attended to all that for us; fact is, this boat is owned by a friend of his, which was how we got it as cheap as we did. And more than that, the gentleman attended to packing all our supplies at the Soo, and sent the boat here on a steamer, so we could start from this place. It was Dr. Philander's idea, you know, this coming through the copper region along the south shore of the Eke. And now, if you're all of the same mind, let's get started."

"Hurrah; hoist the Pennant of the Silver Fox Patrol that your Sister Polly made us, Giraffe, and every fellow dip his hat to the colors of the gay Chippeway Belle!" and in answer to this request on the part of Davy Jones they did salute the raising of the neat little burgee that had a silver fox fashioned in silken hand-work upon it.

Thad examined the engine carefully. He knew considerable about such things, and yet he fancied, he might have more or less trouble with the motive power of this Lake Superior boat; for it was of rather an ancient pattern, and had evidently seen its best days.

Between them Thad and Allan confessed this much, but they did not think it good policy to say anything to the others, though anxious Bumpus watched their conference uneasily, and could be seen to carefully pick out a spot on the rail where he perched, and seemed inclined to stay—it was handy to a quick getaway in case the worst happened, and the engine blew up, as he whispered to himself.

After he had, as he believed, mastered the rudiments of the working of the motor Thad told them to cast off, and they would make a start. Several men stood around to watch them get away, among them the party in whose charge the boat had been left, and who had only delivered it up after Thad had produced an order for the same, and paid certain expenses for storage and watching.

"Were moving at last!" called Step Hen excitedly, as the machinery started to go with a rush, after Thad had cranked the engine.

Allan stood by the wheel, and as the prow of the boat gurgled through the clear waters of the great lake, every scout was thrilled with the vast possibilities that faced them, now that their cruise had begun.

"This means that we'll eat our first meal aboard at noon to-day," remarked Giraffe who seemed determined that no regular feeding time might be neglected, if he could help it.

"You ought to be a happy fellow, Giraffe," remarked Davy Jones, "after taking a look over the piles of grub we've got aboard. Why, do you know there's a whole big ham, two slabs of bacon, and all sorts of good things. No danger of any of us going hungry on this excursion; unless the old tub should happen to sink, and leave us marooned on some rocky island."

"Oh! see here, stop joking about that sort of thing, Davy," remonstrated Bumpus, shivering as though he felt a cold draught; "I know right well that if such a horrible thing ever did happen to us, the rest of you'd make up your minds to begin on me the first thing."

"Well, that's the penalty you have to pay, Bum, pus, for being so tempting," chuckled Step Hen; "now, who'd ever think of picking Giraffe out for a dainty meal; why he's as skinny as an old crow."

"There are times when it pays right well to be thin," remarked the scout held up to derision, "and that'd be one of 'em, I reckon."

They were by now far away from the ore dock, and the barges that were loading; indeed it was only with an effort they could see either, for a haze had crept over the surface of the lake. The Chippeway Belle had been going along at quite a fair pace, thought making more noise than was agreeable to either Thad or Allan, when all at once, without the least warning there was heard a loud report. Instantly the sound of the engine ceased.

"She's broke down, and we're wrecked already!" yelled Giraffe, excitedly.

"Oh! mercy! and she may explode at any second now!" cried poor Bumpus; after which, in sheer desperation he jumped deliberately overboard, clinging to the side of the swaying craft, and in momentary expectation of hearing a fearful crash, as the gasoline tank went up.

CHAPTER V

THE RESCUE

"Tell us what to do, Thad, and count on us to follow you!" called out Giraffe, rising manfully to the occasion; though to tell the honest truth he looked pretty "white around the gills," as Step Hen remarked later on, when they all found time to compare experiences.

"Just stick to your seats, and don't bother!" was the quick reply Thad sent back.

"Then there ain't any danger?" demanded Davy, drawing the only decent breath he had dared indulge in since that first alarm.

"Not a bit!" called Allan, cheerily.

"And we ain't goin' to have to swim for it then?" Step Hen went on.

"Not unless you feel like taking a bath," replied Thad asked.

"But what happened to our engine?" asked Davy.

"And will we have to pole, or row, the rest of the trip?" proceeded

Giraffe. "I see our finish if that comes around so early in the cruise.

Wow! me to hike through the woods afoot, when it hits a fellow as hard

as this."

"Me too!" sighed Step Hen.

"Oh! don't get excited, boys," remarked Thad, with a broad smile; "no danger of anything like that happening to us just yet. I was half expecting something along these lines to happen; and now that it has, we'll fix that part for keeps. It won't come around again, I promise you that."

"Which isn't saying something else won't," grumbled Giraffe. "The blame old tub is just about ready to go to pieces on us, the first chance she gets; and that's what I think."

"Not so bad as that, Giraffe," remonstrated Thad. "This engine has been a great one in its day."

"Yes, but that day was about away, back in the time of Stephenson," continued the tall scout, who, once he began to complain, could only be shut off with the greatest difficulty.

Everybody seemed to laugh at that, it was so ridiculous; but as Thad was already busily engaged in examining the engine their spirits seemed to rise a little.

"Hey! ain't anybody agoin' to help me in?" piped up a small voice just then, accompanied by a splashing sound.

The boys exchanged looks, and then followed nods, as though like a flash they saw the chance to play something of a Joke on the comrade who was thus appealing for aid.

"Hello! where's the other fellow?" exclaimed Allan, as though he had counted noses, and found one missing.

"That's so, where can he be?" echoed Thad.

"Who's missing?" Thad, went on to say.

"Bob White was only here we'd have him call the toll and find out.

There used to be six kids the bunch."

"It must be Bumpus!" declared Giraffe, solemnly.

"You're right!" said a spluttering voice from some unseen place.

"The poor old silly thing, he just jumped right over into the water without saying Jack Robinson!" Step Hen observed, in such a sad voice you would have thought he was having the tears streaming down his cheeks, when in truth there was a wide grin settled there.

"Oh! then he must surely be drowned," Davy went on to add, in a voice that seemed to be choking with emotion—of some sort.

"I thought I saw the lake rising, and that accounts for it," ventured Step Hen. "When a fellow as big as our poor chum goes down, he displaces just an equal part of water. However will we tell his folks the sad news?"

"Ain't you nearly done all that stuff?" demanded an impatient voice, and there was a rocking motion to the boat; after which a very red face surmounted by a shock of fiery hair, now well plastered down, hove in sight. "Hey! somebody get a move on, and give me a hand. I'm soaked through and through, and I tell you my clothes weigh nigh on three tons."

The five boys pretended to be hardly able to believe their eyes. They threw up their hands, and stared hard at the apparition.

"Why, sure, I believe it's our long lost chum, Bumpus!" gasped Giraffe.

"Mebbe it's his ghost come back to haunt us the rest o' out lives. Mebbe we better knock him on the head; they say that's the only sure way to settle spooks," and as Step Hen said this terrible thing, he started to pick up the long-handled boat book.

26

"No, you don't, Step Hen!" shrilled Bumpus, who was really frightened as long as he remained in the water, for he believed it must be a mile deep so far out from land. "You just put that pole down, and get hold of my arm here. I tell you I'm tired of being in soak so long, and I want to come aboard so's to get some dry duds on. Make 'em behave, Thad, can't you? I'm getting weak holding on here all this while; and pretty soon I'll have to let go. Then there will be a ghost, sure, to haunt this crowd. Ain't you coming to assist a fellow scout in distress?"

Realizing that the joke had gone far enough the scout-master himself sprang forward to give poor Bumpus the assistance he craved.

There was no lack of help after that, Step Hen even made use of the boat hook to take hold of some part of the wet scout's clothes; and with a mighty "heave-o!" they dragged him, puffing, and shedding gallons of water, on to the deck of the stalled power-boat. Here he lay for a minute or two "to drain," as Giraffe remarked, but soon feeling chilled, Bumpus began to hunt for his clothes-bag in order to get something dry to put on.

As he did not have a complete outfit for a change, the other fellows helped out; but while his soaked khaki suit was drying, hanging here and there so the sun could do the business, the fat scout presented a laughable appearance, since of course none of the things that had been so generously loaned him began to fit his stout figure.

However, since Bumpus was by nature a jolly chap, he quickly saw the humor of the thing. This was after he had become warmed up fairly well, when he could sit and watch those who were tinkering with the broken engine, and tell what his feelings were as he sprang so hurriedly over into the big lake.

It made him shiver, though, to look around at that sea of water, and realize what an exceedingly reckless boy he had been.

"Next time anything happens, me to stick to the old boat, even if I go up a mile high in the air!" he declared, raising his right hand solemnly, as though taking a vow.

"Have your wings ready, Bumpus, and you'll be all right, because you can fly," said Giraffe; and that provoked another laugh; because Bumpus, once upon a time, being very ambitious to learn how to swim, had purchased a pair of those "White Wings," which are simply bags made of waterproof cloth that can be inflated, and used after the manner of life preservers; so that he had had heaps of fun poked at him on account of his "wings."

So a full hour passed.

Some of the boys were growing impatient, and to relieve the monotony, Thad managed to call the attention of Giraffe to the fact that it lacked only ten minutes of high noon.

That was enough.

"I thought I was feeling pretty weak!" ex-claimed the tall scout, rubbing his stomach sympathetically, "and no wonder, with breakfast so far back I've even clean forgot what I had. Come along, boys, let's get busy with lunch."

"The rest of you can attend to that," said Thad, satisfied that his plan had worked; "and by the time you are ready to call us, we'll have this job all done, so we can start her going."

That was cheering news, and the rest immediately set to work with a will. There was a little stove aboard that used gasoline for fuel, and with this it seemed as though they ought to be able to do all the cooking they wanted when away from land. Of course should they have the opportunity, they meant to go ashore many times, and have one of the old-fashioned camp-fires, around which they had sat so many times in the past, when on their outings.

Before long the smell of cooking that filled the air told that the laborers were making a success of the warm lunch business. Bumpus in particular seemed fairly wild for things to get done.

"I tell you, I just can't seem to get any warmth inside me," he complained when Step Hen took him to task for showing such unusual impatience. "That water was as cold as Greenland, and went right through me. I want my coffee, and I know when I want it."

"Guess your being so badly scared had a heap to do with it," remarked

Giraffe.

"Perhaps so, Giraffe," replied the fat scout, meekly; "I admit that I was frightened out of a year's growth, because I once dreamed I was burned in just such an accident as a boat taking fire. But how about you, Giraffe? The first time my head came up above the coming of the deck I saw your face, and say, talk to me about a gravestone being white, that wasn't anything alongside your phiz."

"You don't say!" jeered the tall scout, though he looked conscious of the fact that his face was now as red as a beet.

"And chances are that you didn't jump the same way I did because you were scared so bad you just couldn't move a finger," Bumpus went on, seeing his advantage.

28

"Thad!" called out Giraffe, scorning to pay attention to the thrust.

"All right!" answered the other.

"Lunch ready!" Giraffe went on to say.

"And so is our job done," saying this Thad I gave the crank a quick turn, upon which there was a quick response; for the merry popping of the engine greeted the anxious ears of the young cruisers.

"Hurrah!" shouted Bumpus, who was feeling fine, now that he had given Giraffe a return jab, after having it rubbed in so hard by the tall scout.

The Chippeway Belle was already moving rapidly through the water, rising and falling on the waves that came out of the southwest; and as the six lads gathered around to do justice to the spread that was to serve as their first meal afloat, they once more saw things in a cheery light, for all seemed going well with them.

CHAPTER VI

THE RIVAL FISHERMEN

As the afternoon crept on, and the boat continued to keep up a merry pace, the boys began to feel their confidence return. As Thad assured them he did not expect to have any further trouble with the engine, they no longer kept an anxious eye on the working part of the craft, while at the least unusual sound every fellow's heart seemed ready to jump into his throat with wild alarm.

It was not the purpose of the cruisers to try and cross the vast body of water upon which their little craft was launched, and which is so immense that for two whole days they might be out of sight of land. Thad knew the danger that lay in such a thing, and had promised the folks at home in Cranford that he would be very careful. Indeed, only for the presence of Dr. Hobbs, some of the parents of the scouts might have felt like revoking their promise to allow their boys to be of the party.

Accordingly their course was now laid in such a quarter that they could keep the land in sight upon their port quarter most of the time.

Of course, while the scouts had not been at sea, and really knew very little of navigation, they were ambitious to learn. And as Bumpus had before hand written down all sorts of phrases used long ago on board the ships that sailed the seas in such white-winged flocks before the advent of steam gave them such a backset, he read these all out to his mates; and after that, whenever they could think of the nautical name for anything they insisted on using it, because, as Giraffe declared, it gave such a realistic effect to things.

"But let me tell you there's a rumpus in the navy these days," said Step Hen, as Giraffe asked him to "step aft, and hand me that pair of binoculars, so I can take an observation."

"What about?" asked Thad.

"Why, they want to abolish some of these old terms that are just a part of sea-faring life. For instance they say that when the man at the wheel is told to 'port your helm,' it takes just the fraction of a second for it to pass through his mind that that means 'turn your helm to the left.' And so they say in our navy after this the officer will callout: 'Turn your helm to the left, Jack!' Whew! that must rile every old jack tar, though. It's like taking the seasoning out of the mince meat."

"Don't you believe it'll ever pass," asserted Bumpus, indignantly; "and just after I've made up my mind to learn every one of this list so I can rattle it off like I can already box the compass. No siree, every true sailorman will rise up in arms against it. You can count on my vote in favor of sticking to the old way. Nothing like the old things, say!"

"'Cepting engines," interposed Step Hen, maliciously.

"Oh! well, I draw the line there, that's true," Bumpus admitted, with a shrug of his fat shoulders, as his eyes unconsciously dropped, so that he looked down into the depths of the lake, "a full mile deep," as he always said to himself.

"Oh! I saw a fish then!" he suddenly shouted, showing new excitement.

"Get your hook and line, Bumpus, and mebbe we'll have fried speckled trout or white fish for supper!" remarked Giraffe, with what he meant to be satire in his speech.

"Huh! I ain't that green about fishing, and you know it," remarked the other, as he gave the tall scout a look of scorn. "Anyhow, I can beat you a mile fishing any day in the week, Giraffe, and I don't care who hears me say it."

"Is that a challenge, Bumpus?" demanded Thad, seeing a chance for some fun to enliven their cruise.

"If he chooses to take me up, you can call it that," responded the fat boy, with a belligerent look at his rival.

"Oh! I'm ready to meet you half way, Bumpus; anything to oblige," Giraffe went on to say, sturdily. "I'd just like a good chance to show you up for a fish fakir. We've heard a heap about how you used to haul 'em in; now's your chance to prove that you're the big gun of this trip."

"All right, just as you say, and we'll leave it to Thad to lay down the terms of the contest, the loser to treat the crowd to a dinner when we get back home," Bumpus went on to say, with the took of one who would die sooner than give up.

"No need of that last," Allan asserted, with a shake of his head. "We expect to have a spread anyhow when we arrive back in Cranford, because there's plenty of money in the treasury of the Silver Fox Patrol; but the loser must do the drudgery that always goes with a dinner, and be the waiter for the other seven fellows. Do you both agree to that?"

"I do!" said Bumpus, holding up his right hand, just as thought he might be before Squire Jasper, and about to give his evidence in court.

"Ditto here; I agree, Thad," Giraffe hastened to say, not wishing to have it appear that he lagged behind his competitor a particle.

"Now, about the terms; what sort of fish are we to grab?" Bumpus wanted to know.

"You don't grab any, Bumpus," Giraffe warned him; "every one must be fairly caught with hook and line, and no seines or nets or guns used. Ain't that right, judge?"

Thad immediately declared he understood that, it was to be a genuine sportsmanlike proceeding, and that no underhand tactics would be tolerated.

"First the number will count," he went on to explain; "after that variety will stand for a second point. Then the heaviest fish will be a third claim, and we might as well make it interesting, so let's call the smallest fish caught a fourth point."

"That's four in all; can't you think up another, so's to have it five; and then three points will be a majority, and wins out?" suggested Davy Jones.

"A good idea, Davy," Thad assured him; "suppose, then, we also say the longest fish when measured by inches; that would make five points, all right."

"Yes," interrupted Giraffe, "but ain't that already covered when you say the biggest fish?"

"Not necessarily," Thad told him, "though in some cases the two would go together, I suppose. But sometimes you'll catch a bass that measures two inches longer than the one the other fellow got, but when you use the scales his weighs more by six ounces. How does that come—well, we've got an illustration right here in you and Bumpus; you call yourself the larger by nearly a foot, but when it comes—"

Giraffe threw up his hands in token of surrender.

"That's right, Thad," declared Bumpus, "the longest ain't always high notch. They do say the best goods come in the smallest packages. But write the conditions down, Thad, while they're fresh in our minds, and read 'em out. When I come in under the wire first, as I surely will, it'd grieve me to hear any squealing from our tall friend here, and have any dispute about not understanding the rules of the game."

Giraffe sniffed scornfully, but did not say anything. However, for a long time after that both boys busied themselves sorting out the greatest lot of fishing tackle their chums had seen for an age; showing that they were in deadly earnest about trying to win the wager.

Bumpus even managed to attach a phantom minnow to the end of a line, which he slyly dropped overboard when he thought no one was looking, in hopes of being fortunate enough to get first blood in the competition. And the others knew that if this thing kept up they were bound to have plenty of fun in watching the desperate efforts of the rival fishermen.

Thad was looking up at the sky occasionally.

"Seem to be some clouds gathering?" remarked Allan, noticing this action on the part of the pilot of the expedition.

"Yes, but then they may not mean anything; though I've been told that storms do come up very suddenly around here. May be something about this big body of fresh water that brings that about, for the sun must draw heaps up from Old Superior every hot day."

"I reckon, now, you're aiming to get to that cove you marked on the chart, so's to have a snug harbor for the night," Allan went on to say.

"Just what I am," the other admitted; "this lake is a bit too big for us to think of anchoring out, and taking chances. A storm is bad enough in daytime when you can see around you; but it must be terrible in the pitch darkness."

"Excuse me, if you please," spoke up Step Hen, who had been listening to all the others said. "I hope there are aplenty of them same snug harbors; for a boat the size of ours to drop in and stay overnight."

"That's just the trouble about cruising on Superior," said Thad, "and especially along the American shore, because there are few rivers that empty into the lake. Up along the Canadian side it's different, because there are some fine trout streams that extend from White Fish Bay along toward old Fort William."

"I'd like to see that last place," spoke up Davy, "because I've heard about it ever since I was knee high to a grasshopper. You see, my great grandfather used to live in Montreal in the days when the Northwest Fur Company was in competition with the Hudson Bay Company, and my ancestor was employed each Spring to set out from Montreal with some, big batteaus manned by French Canadian voyageurs, who would row and sail all the way through most of the Great Lakes to Fort William, where the agent had collected heaps of valuable pelts from the trappers and the Injuns after the season was done. These he'd fetch all the way back to Montreal again, the flat bottom boats being loaded down with the bales. And let me tell you that was taking risks some; but they raised men in them days, I reckon, men that never allowed themselves to think of such a thing as danger, because they were always facing some sort of perils."

33

"I guess you're, about right, Davy," admitted Thad; "and I often sit and wonder how it'd seem if a fellow lived away back in those days before the times of automobiles, motorboats, telephones, talking machines and electricity."

"Huh!" grunted Bumpus, "according to my mind, what dangers they faced ain't to be mentioned in the same breath as them we have hovering over us all the while. For instance, what if Thad here just crooked his hand, wouldn't we be apt to run smack into that other boat that's goin' to pass us right now.

"And say, fellows," remarked Giraffe, in a low, mysterious tone, that somehow managed to thrill the others, as no doubt he intended it should; "just take a peek at the men in that boat, will you? Somehow I don't know just why, but they make me think of pirates, if ever they have such critters up here on Old Superior. And take it from me, boys, right now one of the bunch is looking us over through a marine glass. Like as not they're making up their minds who and what we can be, and if it's going to pay 'em to board this same craft, to clean it out. Don't anybody make out like we're watching 'em; but try and remember where you put our gun, Thad; because who knows but what we might need the same right bad before long?"

CHAPTER VII

"Gee! Pirates! Whew!"

That was only Bumpus talking to himself; as he lay there on the deck, and stared across the swelling water toward the black powerboat that was heading the other way, so as to cross their course.

There were apparently several men in the strange boat; and as Giraffe had just remarked, they seemed to be more or less interested in the Chippeway Belle and her young crew, for every one of them was looking that way, and one man really had a pair of marine glasses up to his eyes.

Thad dived into the interior of what was called the "hunting cabin," and quickly reappeared bearing the glasses they had been wise enough to fetch along, as well as a compass whereby to steer.

"That's the ticket, Thad!" said Step Hen; "let 'em see they ain't the only pebbles on the beach. We've got a marine glass, too. Now, tell us what you think, are they really lake buccaneers; and will we have to put up a desperate fight to keep from being robbed, and sunk, and perhaps made slaves?"

Bumpus gasped for breath, at hearing such doleful things; but as, Step Hen gave a quick glance toward the fat chum, possibly what he said was only meant to cause the other's flesh to quiver with dread.

"Oh! they don't seem to be altering their course in the least," spoke up Allan; "and as for them watching us, who wouldn't stare on seeing a crowd of boys afloat up here on Superior waters?"

"I was thinking that our uniforms as scouts might make them sit up and take notice," said Giraffe. "P'raps they think we're U. S. soldiers, because the dough-boys all wear this same khaki now instead of the old army blue. And in case they're real bold smugglers or pirates, that would give them cause for a scare. Do they look like they're ready to run away, Thad?"

"Well, not any more than would be the case if they were honest cruisers," replied the other, as he handed the glasses to Allan, who in turn would pass them around. "Seems to me one of them wears some kind of a blue cap, as though he might be an officer of some sort."

"Oh! don't count on that," spoke up Bumpus, "anybody can buy one like that. Ain't I got one right here in my duffel bag; but I hadn't found a chance to spring it on the rest of the bunch. They, may be a tough lot, even if one does wear an officer's cap."

"Well, they're going right along about their own business, and don't seem to be changing their course a little bit," Allan said as he passed the glasses to Giraffe.

"I'm glad to hear that," Bumpus admitted, breathing freely again. "Because, as you all know, I'm very much opposed to violence at any time; though," he continued, "I'd fight if I was hard pushed, and fight real fierce, too."

"We all know that, Bumpus, so there's no need of you apologizing," Thad assured him, with a smile and a nod, for he was very fond of the stout chum.

"But when you said smugglers, what did you mean, Giraffe?" questioned

Step Hen.

"Oh! Don't you know that they have heaps of trouble with such law-breakers all along the Canadian border?" demanded the tall boy. "You see, there's a heavy duty on a lot of things that can come into Canada free, or with only a small sum to pay; and whenever men can make money taking chances, they're just bound to try it. Why, I understand that millions of dollars are lost to the Government every year just in the goods smuggled across the border all the way from Maine to the Pacific ocean."

"Whew! and yonder craft might be one of the tricky boats engaged in that business; is that what you mean, Giraffe?" asked Bumpus, again staring hard after the strange black powerboat which was larger than the Chippeway Belle, and apparently much better able to meet the heavy seas that must sweep across the lake when the wind reached a certain strength.

"Oh! I don't say that, remember," quickly replied the other; "because it's only a guess on my part, and I haven't anything to show for proof. I was just giving you the benefit of a bright thought that came into my brain, that's all. There may be something in it, and again, p'raps them fellows are just a pleasure party; or some sportsmen heading, for a favorite fishing place."

"Then if we followed 'em, we'd stand a show to find where the fish lie," suggested Bumpus; showing that at least he had not forgotten about his recent wager, even in the midst of all this excitement.

"Better mind your own business, I think," remarked Allan.

"Yes," added Giraffe, "if so be they turned out to be a bad lot, they'd think we kept poking our noses in just to arrest them; and in that case chances are we'd get our fingers burned."

"But what do you think they might be, Thad?" persisted Step Hen, noticing that the pilot of the expedition had as yet not given any opinion on the matter.

"Oh! any one of the explanations you fellows have put up might cover the bill," Thad, went on to say. "The idea came into my mind that perhaps now those men might be game-fish wardens."

"W-what!" gasped Bumpus; "d'ye mean to tell me they have such things on a big lake like this? Why, I thought they were only needed ashore, where ponds and rivers require looking after."

"That's where you make a big mistake," Thad informed him. "Right up among the Great Lakes there are millions of dollars taken out in fish every year; and if the Government didn't watch sharp plenty of unscrupulous fishermen would use all kinds of illegal devices for getting big hauls. They are limited to certain kinds of nets or seines; and so the precious sturgeon, and the delicious white fish that are in these lakes will be kept from being exterminated."

"Thank you for telling us that, Thad; it's all news to me," said Step Hen. "But what about the trout; I've heard there are awful big speckled trout in Superior?"

"So there are, as high as eight pounds; and the Government hatchery at the Soo has hundreds that large in their ponds, for breeding purposes, I've read," Thad continued, for the topic was a favorite one with him, and he was a very accommodating boy at that; "that in Michigan, for instance, the law doesn't allow trout to be offered for sale or shipped; so while they catch some whoppers in the acts they use for white fish, they have to put most of them back."

"And then you think that p'raps those men are wardens, looking for poachers that are breaking the law some way or other?" Giraffe asked.

"I only said that might be who they are," Thad insisted. "You notice they have a high-powered boat that could make circles all around, ours, if they wanted to let her engine out. And it's painted black, perhaps so they can sneak up on a dark night without being seen. But as they're two miles away from us by now, suppose we cut out talking any more about them."

From the way Thad turned his eyes upward, and looked at the gathering clouds it was evident that he felt he had better pay attention to other matters which threatened to cause them more or less annoyance before long.

37

The wind was certainly freshening very fast. And of necessity the waves began to take on a size that made poor Bumpus stare, and look serious, as he contemplated the possibility of a wreck.

"Sure you are heading right to make that cove?" Giraffe asked the skipper who had the wheel in his charge.

The engine was plodding away steadily, though some of the boys were worried at the quick whirr that followed the passing of each big wave, when, perhaps the propeller would be partly exposed, and the resistance so much less that it spun around, much faster than usual.

"Yes, no doubt about it at all, and if everything goes along right we stand to make our harbor before dark comes along," the other answered.

"Oh! I wish we were there already," groaned Bumpus; and when Thad looked at the fat scout he noticed how white he was.

But then that was nothing singular, for it was certainly getting pretty rough out there on that great expanse of water, and some of the scouts were sure to display signs of seasickness sooner or later, he knew. Perhaps poor Bumpus was fated to be the first victim.

"Well," remarked Giraffe, trying hard to appear indifferent, though he could not wholly hide his concern every time a wave larger than ordinary would slap against the side of the boat, and sweep along toward the stern, causing a quiver to run all through the little craft that seemed just like a chip on that inland sea; "I reckon now, it would be pretty tough if we missed connections somehow, and had to keep marking time all night long out on this old bathtub."

"Oh! Murder! I hope we don't!" muttered Bumpus, shivering.

"Stop that kind of talk, Giraffe," ordered Thad, who would rather look on the bright side of things; "don't you see you're only bothering Bumpus?"

"There's no need of feeling that we're going to have trouble; because the engine is working as fine as silk right now, and I feel sure I can see where that same jolly little cove lies, away ahead there."

"You mean where that small point juts out, don't you, Thad?" asked Allan, who hovered constantly near his best chum, ready to take a hand at a second's notice, should there ever arise an occasion calling for assistance.

"Yes, that shows on the Government chart I've marked, and the cove lies just in the shelter of it. I think a little river makes into the lake there, and if so we might pick up some fish before starting out again."

He spoke this loud enough for Bumpus to hear; but apparently that sad individual had lost all interest in the wager he had so recently made with Giraffe, for he did not take any notice of what Thad said, only continued to look far away, and press his hand up and down in the pit of his stomach; and when a boy begins to realize that he has such an organ at all, he must be in a pretty bad way.

Still the wind kept on increasing until it was blowing a small gale. Even the confident Thad felt a little nervous as he wondered what would happen should their engine suddenly give a groan and cease to labor. The situation must be anything but pleasant, left at the mercy of the coming storm, out there a couple of miles from the southern shore, and further than that away from the lovely little cove where they had hoped to pass the night in peace and safety.

The next half hour was apt to settle that matter, one way or the other; and of course Thad found no reason to despair, as yet, for the motor kept buzzing away cheerily, and the boat pushed through the rising and falling, billows quite sturdily, as the pilot kept her pointed toward that headland far beyond.

CHAPTER VIII

NO END OF TROUBLES

"What's that queer sound?" asked Step Hen, looking up suddenly.

"Oh, never mind, it's only me," came from the side of the boat, where

Bumpus was lying flat on his stomach, and leaning over.

The boys looked at each other; perhaps Thad and Allan smiled somewhat, but for a wonder none of the others had any kind of joke to spring just then; for truth to tell Giraffe, Davy and even Step Hen himself were feeling as though if this sort of swaying motion had to keep up much longer they could not resist the temptation to copy after the boy who was so terribly seasick.

"Thought I felt a drop of rain just then," remarked Giraffe, more to have something to talk about, and so forget his other troubles, than that he really believed it.

"No, it must only have been the spray," said Thad. "You notice that sometimes after a big wave slaps up against our larboard quarter, the wind carries drops of water flying past. It's a lively little blow all right, though I suppose the people up here, who are used to much worse things, wouldn't think this anything."

"P'raps they might if they were out so far from land, in such a little pumpkinseed of a boat," complained Step Hen.

"And with an old rattletrap of a motor that's threatening to wheeze its last any minute, at that," added Giraffe, fiercely.

"Let up on that kind of talk, Giraffe," said Davy; "we've sure all got troubles of our own as it is, without that silly calling of names. For my part I think the engine is doing its prettiest, and I take off my hat to it. Don't, you go to calling it hard names, or it might get even by kicking over the traces, and quitting on us. Then we would be in a fine pickle. But I think it's better to keep lying down, all you can, when it blows like this. Make room there, Bumpus, can't you?"

Then there were two of them; and talk about your rivalry, it did seem as though both of those fellows would tear themselves to pieces, as the boat continued to swing up and down with that perpetual sickening, nauseating movement.

Presently Step Hen found a place too, and tried to outdo his comrades; seeing which Giraffe apparently thought he might as well make it unanimous then there were four, leaving only the skipper and his first assistant on deck to manage the boat.

"Anyhow, the cargo will be lighter after all this," Giraffe spoke up, after a while, showing that even seasickness could not quite extinguish his love of joking.

By now they had covered considerable distance, so that the little headland loomed not a great away beyond.

Thad, too, had changed their course somewhat, so that they were now much closer shore than before; and unless some accident happened he believed that before another twenty minutes passed they would be able to get the shelter of that projecting tongue of land, after which their present troubles would fade away.

It was time, too, for already the first dim signs of coming darkness could be seen around them; no doubt the fact that clouds covered the face of the sky had more or less to do with this early closing in of the night, as is always the case.

Bumpus was sitting up, though looking very white indeed. Every now and then he would shake his round head in a doleful way, and heave a tremendous sigh, as though he might be wondering if his whole past would be appearing before him, since, as he complainingly told the sympathizing Thad, "everything seemed to be coming up nowadays."

"Only a little while ago I was worrying my poor old head off for fear the boat would sink with me," he went on to say, with a dismal smile; "and now it's just the other way, and I'm feelin' bad because she won't sink."

"Oh! don't let yourself down like that, Bumpus," said Allan; "we're going in behind that headland right away, and you'll be surprised to see how quick you get over feeling bad. There, the water isn't near so rough as it was, right now; and soon it'll seem like a mill pond."

"Do you think so; wish I could believe it?" called out Step Hen, without turning his head, for he was very busy; "but seems to me the old boat is jumping as bad as any cayuse I ever saw, when we were out in the Wild West. Oh!"

All the same Allan was right, for they were passing in behind the projecting tongue of land, and already the worst was over, for the seas were not near so heavy, though of course the change was hardly noticeable to those who were feeling so badly.

And so it came about that presently Thad had to lessen their speed, for he did not want to run aground, or have any other accident occur that would cripple the boat, and shorten their cruise.

"We're all right, now, fellows," sang out Giraffe, being the first to recover, simply because he had more grit and determination than any of the other three who had been knocked out by the motion of the craft in the big seas.

"Yes, and our next job is to prowl around here some, before dark gets us, so as to find the best anchorage," Thad remarked, as the boat crept slowly along back of the point.

"Why, I should think any place here would answer," said Giraffe; "because that wind from the southwest ain't going to get a whack at us any longer."

"But who'll guarantee that the wind doesn't shift into the north during the night, and have a full sweep at us here?" asked Thad. "No, we ought to find out if there really is a little stream flowing into the lake here; and if so the mouth of that same will afford us the safest place to anchor, or tie up."

"I agree with you there, Thad," said Bumpus, weakly; but then the fact that he took any sort of interest in what was going on announced plainly enough that he must be recovering.

And the others had by this time reached their limit, for they contributed no more to the fishes of Superior, but began to sit up, and take notice of things. The recovery from seasickness is usually as rapid as the coming of the trouble; given a firm foundation to stand upon, and the sufferer soon forgets his agony, so that he can even remember that food tastes good.

Pushing their way carefully in the scouts presently discovered that there was a stream of some kind emptying into the lake at this place; and that around several bends there was a splendid anchorage for a small boat such as theirs, though a larger craft might find some difficulty about getting in, on account of shallow water.

And when they dropped their anchor over at last, all of them were pleased to feel that they had left that riotous sea behind them.

"This is something like," declared Giraffe, now fully recovered, and of course sharp set to get supper started; indeed all of them felt as though they could do ample justice to a good meal.

So the gasoline stove was put into service again, and everyone helped get the things ready that their menu for that night called for. Giraffe started a pot of rice cooking, for he was very fond of that dish, and could "make a meal off it," he often declared; though his chums noticed that even when he had plenty of the same beside him, he dipped into every other dish just as usual.

Besides this one of the boys opened a large tin of corned beef that was emptied into a kettle, together with a can of corn, and another of lima beans, the whole making what is known as a "canoeist's stew," and is not only tasty to the hungry voyager, but exceedingly filling as well.

These, with crackers, cheese, some cakes done up in air-proof packages, and tea constituted the supper that was finally placed before them.

It really seemed to some of those hungry boys as though that was the finest feast they had ever sat down to. Of course that often came to their minds, because what they were just then eating tasted so very good. But with such enormous appetites as a sauce, there could never be any chance for a complaint coming. And the chief cook received so many compliments that it was no wonder his cheeks and ears burned like the fire he had been standing over so long.

By the time the meal was through it was very dark all around them. They could still hear the wind blowing out beyond the point; and the wash of the big waves told that the sea was probably higher than before; so that every fellow expressed himself as glad that they had managed to get into such a splendid harbor, where they need not bother their minds what sort of weather held outside.

The night was warm, and it seemed comfortable enough for them to lie around on the deck, exchanging comments. Later on they would arrange just how they were to pile into that small cabin, and manage to sleep; for six boys can take up considerable room; and there would have been even seven to fill the space had not the scout-master, Dr. Hobbs, been recalled home at the last moment.

Of course Bumpus had entirely recovered from his indisposition. He only hoped he would now be proof against a second attack.

In fact, he had even begun to remember the terms of the wager, and was trying to get a line out on the sly, baited with a piece of meat he had fastened to the hook, in hopes of some gullible fish taking hold, so that he could wildly haul his captive in, and have the laugh on his competitor.

When morning came he was determined to go ashore, and see if he could not find some angle worms; for without bait it was folly to think of catching fish on hooks; and all sorts of other contraptions were barred from the contest.

Giraffe, however, was not asleep, and he saw what his rival was up to; but although Bumpus was not aware of the fact, the tall scout had had his line over the side for half an hour now, also baited, and with the hope of a bite.

From now on the race promised to become pretty warm between them, once they got fully started in the game.

They had talked over about every subject that could be imagined, including the matter of the mysterious powerboat that had passed them that afternoon, apparently heading in another direction; though Thad knew that long afterwards those in the black craft had altered their course, and were really following them.

It was getting along near time when they ought to be thinking about retiring so as to get some rest, when another subject came up suddenly.

Giraffe, who had been stretching that long neck of his for some little time, observed that he was trying to make out what a certain queer light might stand for.

"It's away up the shore yonder, fellows, and seems to be a lantern, as near as I can make out," he went on to say; "every now and then it bobs up, and down; and if you asked me I'd say it was, meant for some sort of signal!"

"A signal!" echoed Bumpus, in almost an awed tone; "that sounds like there might be smugglers, or something, like that around here; and perhaps they take us for revenue officers trying to nip them at their work. Whew! spells more trouble for us, I'm afraid. First the storm; then that awful spell of gone feeling; and now it's smugglers. Whew! I say!"

CHAPTER IX

"BE PREPARED!"

Bumpus was not the only fellow who felt his heart beating much faster than its wont just then, though none of the others betrayed the fact; for Giraffe and Step Hen were too crafty to show that they were worried.

They seemed to be in a trap, for the heavy seas would not allow them to think of leaving their anchorage until morning came along, at least; and to remain might be exposing themselves to some unknown peril.

But then these lads had done through so many things, especially since they joined the Cranford Troop of Boy Scouts, and learned what it meant to think for themselves, that none of them really displayed the white feather, no matter if Bumpus, who loved peace so much that he sometimes fought to secure it, did manifest some uneasiness.

They had along with them a double-barreled shotgun that had always given a good account, of itself in times past; and would again if called to show its sterling qualities. And with this in the hands of Thad Brewster, who was a perfectly fearless chap, according to his churns, who did not know that his boy heart could hammer in his breast like a runaway steam engine, why, they surely ought to be able to stave off any ordinary attack.

Giraffe felt better when he had picked up the camp hatchet, and waved it several times in the air, making vicious stabs at an imaginary enemy.

"Get ready for boarders, fellows!" remarked Step Hen, who had reached in and secured the long bread-knife, which would make a most formidable weapon, if only he had the nerve to wield the same.

"Not on your life!" snapped Giraffe; "we've got enough mouths to feed as it is, without taking, on any more. Boarders nothing. You've got another think coming, Step Hen, don't you see?"

"But after all, fellows," Thad told his followers, "this may be a false alarm. That light has gone now. It may only have been some farmer or miner letting his wife know he was on the way home. How do we know any different? And what interest would any rascals have in trying to come aboard this boat?"

"That sounds all very fine, Thad," remarked Davy; "but I hope we ain't thinkin' of all going to sleep at once to-night!"

"We ought to have a sentry on duty all the time," suggested Giraffe.

"I appoint you for that onerous duty, then, Giraffe; consider that settled," the scout-master said, like a flash; whereupon the tall chap began to hedge, and explain more fully his views.

"Oh! course I didn't mean that one scout should sit up all night," he went on to remark; "but by taking turns we'd feel that the boat wasn't agoing to be carried off while we slept. Sure I'm willing to stand my turn, which might be any two hours you set; and then I'll wake up the next man. You know we've done that same many a time when we were up in Maine, down along the Blue Ridge, and out among the Rockies hunting big game."

"Of course I understood what you meant, Giraffe," the scout-master went on to remark; "and as you say, some of us will spell you, a new man going on duty every two hours. But I hope now nobody really believes that we're going to be attacked, by lake pirates, or smugglers, or anything like that. Those who lie down to sleep, just forget everything. We're safe here in a splendid harbor and nothing will happen to bother us."

"But if it should, Thad, you'll wake us all up, I hope," urged Bumpus.

"I promise you that, Bumpus," returned Thad; "because I know just how you feel about it. No fellow likes to be kicked while he's asleep; with his eyes open he's in a way to take care of himself. Oh! Yes, we'll see that every one is waked up if there's going to be a row; because we'll have need of your fighting face then, Bumpus, remember."

It was hard to get the fat boy fully aroused, such was his customary good nature; but when he did get beyond the limit, he used to assume what he considered a terrible look, that was supposed to strike fear to the heart of his adversary.

Somehow no one admitted to feeling at all sleepy now. Even Bumpus, who as a rule could be depended on to fall asleep right after he had had his supper, was apparently as wide-awake as a hawk; and joined in all the conversation as they sat around on the deck and waited for, they hardly knew what, to happen.

"Anyhow, we didn't tie up to the shore, as Bumpus wanted when he said he'd feel so much better if he could walk on firm ground again," remarked Step Hen.

"And I'm glad now that twenty feet or more of water lies between us and shore," the party mentioned hastened to add.

"How deep do you think it is in here, Thad?" questioned Davy.

"All of twenty feet in the place our anchor went down," replied the skipper, promptly, "it's a regular hole, such as the trout like to lie in during the hot dog days of late summer."

"Glad to hear you say that," observed Bumpus; but he did not explain whether his pleasure lay in the fact that any would-be boarders might find it difficult to cross over from the rocks to the boat; or that there were likely to be fish in the pool, affording a chance for a nibble at the tempting bait he had dropped overboard, attached to the concealed hook at the end of his line.

"If anybody came along here just on purpose to take a good look at us, whereabouts d'ye think they'd be likely to show up, first of all, Thad?" Step Hen wanted to know.

"I was thinking about that a minute ago, Step Hen," replied the scout-master; "and sort of made up my mind they'd be apt to climb that pile of rocks yonder. You see, it overlooks this pool, and a man might lie there near the top and watch us all he wanted, provided the moon came out, and gave him the light he'd need."

Everybody thereupon cast an eye aloft.

"I'm afraid that moon business is just what's going to happen right soon," observed Giraffe.

"Yes, there isn't going to be a storm after all," remarked the skipper; "clouds are breaking night now, and it was a false alarm, you see."

"Well, hardly, with me," ventured Bumpus; whereupon everybody tittered, because they knew what the fat scout meant; and there were three others, who, if they were as candid as Bumpus, might have added:

"Me too!"

Half an hour passed by, and they were really getting tired, for it was now in the neighborhood of half-past ten o'clock, as Thad told them the last time he consulted his little dollar watch that gave him so much satisfaction in all his outings.

Still, none of them wanted to be the fellow to first crawl under his blanket, it being only a matter of pride that kept Bumpus at least on deck, blinking like an owl in the daytime, as he tried to keep his eyes open.

Jim, by the way, had been fastened to a cleat, and was perched on the edge of the cabin roof, no one as yet daring to touch him; though he had eaten some meat they placed within his reach, which proved that the owl did not mean to starve himself to death, yet awhile at least.

All at once Bumpus felt a galvanic shock.

"Oh!" he shouted in excitement, "it's come at last!"

All the others started up in great alarm.

"What ails the fellow?" cried Step Hen.

47

"Got a fit, I reckon!" echoed Giraffe.

"Fit nothing!" mocked the fat scout, who was bending over, and seemed to be clawing wildly at the air, so that it was no wonder in the darkness they thought he must be having a return engagement with that sea sickness; "I've got a fish, and that's more'n you can claim, Giraffe, with all your smartness!"

"Bah! never count your chicken's till they're hatched!" scoffed the other, as he saw the fat scout suddenly pause, as though there had come a sickening slackening of the line. "Imagination is a great thing, mebbe; but next time be sure of your game before you whoop it up so."

"But he's there yet, I tell you!" ejaculated Bumpus, again becoming active. "Hi! somebody lend me a hand here, so I won't lose him. We need this trout in our business, because we got to have breakfast in the morning."

"Hold on!" said Giraffe, with emphasis; "don't forget that the terms of our wager state distinctly that no one must offer the slightest assistance in landing a fish. If you're after that fish solely for breakfast, why, any of us'll be glad to lend you a hand; but then it don't count. How about that, Thad?"

"You're correct, Giraffe," replied the other; "but I hope Bumpus lands his prize, all right, because fresh fish would taste fine to-morrow morn."

It was a little struggle in the mind of Giraffe as to whether the sportsman spirit, or the love of good feeding would prevail; but at last he also cried out: "I hope he gets it, too, sure I do! Good for you, Giraffe!" exclaimed Thad, perhaps purposely mistaking this for a spirit of fairness that would do the tall scout credit as a true sportsman.

Meanwhile all of them watched Bumpus tugging at his line. The fish was full of fight, and evidently objected to furnishing a breakfast for a party of Boy Scouts off on a vacation cruise; but by sheer strength, and not a little good luck in the bargain rather than fisherman's skill, Bumpus finally man aged to haul his struggling prize aboard.

"It's a trout, as sure as pop!" exclaimed Step Hen, as they all bent over the wiggling and flapping captive, and Giraffe struck a match, the better to see its nature.

"Whee! let me tell you he pulled to beat the band too!" the proud angler vowed, as he rubbed his arms; and then bent lower to admire the spotted sides of the big trout, that probably looked prettier to Bumpus than anything he had ever before seen.

"He's a jim dandy, and that's a fact, Bumpus!" said Giraffe, swallowing his bitter chagrin because fortune had cheated him out of being the first in the contest to bring in such a prize; at the same time he was no doubt thinking what a tasty morsel that splendid fish would afford the lot for breakfast and wondering if there were not several of them who had confessed that they did not care for fish which would allow a larger portion to those who did.

However, all thoughts of this nature were doomed to be forgotten, because just then Davy had to go and throw a bombshell into the camp by remarking in a low and trembling voice:

"Thad, oh Thad! I saw a fellow poke his head up above that pile of rocks just then, give you my word of honor I did!"

"Be prepared!" said the skipper, quickly; and every scout reached out for the weapon he had decided to rely upon in case of dire necessity.

CHAPTER X

THE QUEER WAYS OF BUMPUS

"There ain't a thing moving up there, Davy; and I reckon, now, you're only just afooling us," complained Step Hen, after they had stared as hard as anything at the crown of the rocks, which was sharply outlined against the dark heavens.

As the others had met with like poor success in trying to locate the object the scout in question claimed to have seen, they naturally turned on Davy, to demand further explanations.

It could easily be seen, however, from his excited condition, that the boy actually believed what he said.

When Giraffe and Bumpus, and even Allan, urged him to repeat his assertion, he not only did so, but added still more to what he had said before.

"Guess I ought to know what a man's head looks like, hadn't I?" Davy went on to remark, indignantly; "cause I've seen a few in my day. It was there as plain as—as, well, the nose on my face, and you'll say that's right smart in evidence, I know you will, Giraffe. Looky up yonder—see the little peak that seems to stick up above all the rest of the old rock pile? Well, it was alongside that it showed up; and right while I was asaying it, the thing disappeared like smoke. But you believe me, I saw something, and it was a man's head too, no matter if there was a bear or a panther at the other end of the same."

Strange to say no one chuckled at these queer remarks of Davy. They saw that he was in deadly earnest; and the possibility of a strange man spying on them seemed too serious a matter to arouse a laugh.

"Well," said Step Hen, presently, when they had strained their eyes to the utmost without any result whatever, "seems like he saw you at the same time, and lit out in a big hurry."

Giraffe began to recover from the first shock caused by the alarm; and when he was feeling himself the tall scout could nearly always think of something quaint to say.

"That reminds me of the old baby book rhyme we all used to say; p'raps you'll remember, fellows. It's been a long time since I repeated it, but I think it runs about like this: 'I Saw Esau kissing Kate; and the fact is, we all three saw. I saw Esau, he saw me; and Kate saw I saw Esau.' How's that?"

No one answered, and for a pretty good reason; for hardly had Giraffe uttered his question when, without the slightest warning, a dazzling ray of white light suddenly fell upon the group of scouts crouching there on the after-deck of the little hunting cabin cruiser, causing every one to gasp, and fall to quivering almost as much as though a flash of lightning had darted toward them.

"Oh!" cried some one; and while the tones of the voice could hardly be distinguished on account of the vibration caused by the speaker's alarm, no one had the least doubt but that it was Bumpus who thus betrayed his agitated feelings.

Thad and Allan, and perhaps several of the other scouts, knew instantly that the strong glow was caused by one of those handy little electric torches, for they happened to have just such an alliance along with them, and had made great use of it on numberless occasions.

This told them that after all Davy had spoken truly when he declared so vehemently that he had seen a man's head up there on the rocks.

Nobody moved, only crouched there, staring at that dazzling light, and mentally figuring what was going to happen next.

Doubtless all sorts of alarming theories flitted through their minds, for after their recent talk about smugglers and those sorts of law-breakers the boys were in a good state to imagine things.

They were given very little time, however, to collect their wits; for a gruff voice (strange how voices are always gruff under similar condition but this one was very hoarse without any question) called out:

"Ahoy there, aboard the launch!"

Had it depended on Bumpus, and perhaps Step Hen also, the reply must have been a long time coming, for they hardly dared trust their voices; but then Thad was able to hold his own, and he immediately called back:

"Hello! yourself; what d'ye want?"

"Bring that boat ashore, and be quick about it!" the deep grumble proceeded to tell them; and somehow poor Bumpus was forcibly reminded of the growl of a lion he had once heard in a menagerie, as well as several other things along the same "away down in the cellar" line.

"I suppose we might as well do it, fellows?" Thad remarked to his chums, in somewhat of a low tone; as though he meant to be influenced more or less by what decision the other scouts reached.

"Oh! can't we skip out before they get their hands on us, Thad?" Bumpus wanted to know. "We're full twenty feet and more away from the shore, and it'd take a champion sprinter and jumper to cover that distance."

"Yes, but how about running out into that storm again, eh, Bumpus? Feel like going through another experience like that?" demanded Giraffe.

"Not any for me, thank you. Thad, I say, do what he tells us. He can't eat us, I reckon; and we ain't got any reason to be afraid because of anything we've done."

"Same here, Thad," remarked Davy, quickly: he had been feeling very much like backing up Bumpus in his request, but what Giraffe said caused him to "take water" instantly, and Davy was as quick to make a revolution in his mind as his body could revolve in several handsprings over the ground, when he was feeling good.

"Allan, how about you?" asked Thad, feeling that much depended on what the one addressed thought.

"No help for it, Thad; we've got to throw up our hands that far, anyway; because, like as not they've got us covered right now with their guns, and while they can see us fairly well, everything all dark to us up there."

"Oh! my stars!" Bumpus was heard to whisper to himself, in a horrified tone, as he learned about those terrible firearms that must be held with their muzzles projecting in the direction of the floating home of the scouts; but all the same Bumpus, "though good and scared," as he afterwards candidly confessed, did not attempt to lie down, and shield his round body behind any of his comrades; if they could take the consequences surely he ought to be ready to face the music; and so he only knelt there and quivered and looked, momentarily to see a flash, and hear a deafening report that would stagger them all.

"Well are you going to do what I told you?" the heavy bass voice demanded, more or less, impatiently.

"Don't be so foolish as to think, you can slip away," a second unseen man told them, "because we've got you covered, and if you start up that engine we'll give you a volley that'll make you wish you hadn't. Come ashore with that boat, you hear? We know you, Cranston! The game is up!"

Thad breathed easier, somehow. What had been said seemed to tell him it might after all only be a case of mistaken identity; and that if they obeyed the rough summons they would in all probability not be apt to suffer on account of yielding.

"Get a push pole, somebody, and help me shove ashore!" Thad remarked; and then raising his voice so that the unseen enemies might hear, he continued: "you needn't bother wasting any of your ammunition on us, mister, because, we're willing to do what you, ask, and come to land. So hold up, and give us a chance, for we've got to raise our anchor first; and the water's some deep here to use the poles in."

He heard a low laugh near by, but there was no further comment from those who had the situation well in hand. Every scout understood, however, that a number of heavily armed men must be scrutinizing their actions from the roll; for that strong white glow was kept closely focused on the boat all the time they proceeded to drag in the anchor, and start working the push poles, with which the little hunting cabin launch was well provided.

The water in the harbor they had found was of considerable depth, but fortunately the poles were long as well as stout, and presently the boat began to move slowly in response to the energetic efforts which Thad and Giraffe put forth.

Bumpus had assisted to pull in the anchor, and was now squatted like a big frog near the bow. He knew full well that his position was very much exposed, and that in case the unseen enemy chose to actually open fire upon the boat, he would likely be the first to suffer; but in spite of this Bumpus refused to budge. He had gotten over his first qualms of fear, and feeling ashamed of allowing himself to give way to such a sensation, and he a scout in the bargain, the boy was now going to the other extreme, and growing actually reckless.

It made him think of the time some of his mates had declared they had seen a real boni-fide ghost in the town graveyard, and dared Bumpus to lead the way in there, late at night, when they were passing. He had felt his teeth rattle together, just as they had been doing now; but summoning all his courage to the fore he had grimly said: "who's afraid?" and trembling like a leaf shaken in the wind, he had stalked into the cemetery, much to the admiration of his chums, who had expected the fat boy to back down abjectly.

The boat approached the shore slowly.

Thad could not exactly see the forms of those who were waiting for them to come in, but since the focus of light changed from spot to spot he concluded that they were also drawing closer to the shore line, so as to be ready to receive those whom they already counted on as their prisoners.

And, Thad waited, in momentary expectation of hearing some sort of explosion, when the parties realized their mistake. In fact, he was so sure of this that he would not make the slightest effort to draw that shotgun closer to him, though that might have seemed good policy.

Finally the nose of the cruiser came smack up against the rocks with quite a little bump; and Giraffe, having failed to fend off in time, was almost toppled over, but he managed to clutch hold of Bumpus to steady himself, and that was like seizing upon the Rock of Gibraltar, because it would take a derrick to move the stout scout, once he settled down.

So, when for the second time the boat came in contact with the shore,

Giraffe was able to give a little leap, painter in hand, and reach land.

Just as he did so, that deep bus voice sprang up again; and this time, as Thad had expected, it told of considerable chagrin and disappointment.

"Well, what's this? Only a bunch of kids, after all, instead of Cranston and his gang of smugglers. The joke's on us, men; it is to laugh!"

CHAPTER XI

THE FAME OF THE SILVER FOX PATROL

"I thought so!" Thad now remarked, showing what confidence he had felt in the decision that their best policy had been to obey orders, and come to the shore.

Several moving figures were now seen, and coming down the rocks toward them. In another minute's time these had resolved themselves into three men. They did not seem to be roughly dressed at all, but might be taken for gentlemen out to have a good time fishing or cruising.

And the boys noticed, as soon as they could see anything at all, when Thad lighted their camp lantern, that the largest of the trio wore a blue cap such as they had seen on the head of the man who watched their boat through his field-glasses late that afternoon.

Undoubtedly the black boat had turned back as evening set in, and it must have been some one connected with the party, whom they had seen waving that light from the shore.

"Good evening!" said Allan, pleasantly, as the three men ranged up close by and evidently looked them over; "we've surrendered, you remember. Now, what are you going to do with six Boy Scouts off for a vacation trip on the lake?"

At that the big man turned to his companions, and laughed. No doubt they felt considerably disappointed, because they had somehow had high hopes of making an important capture; but after the first keen chagrin had passed they could enjoy a joke at their own expense.

"You'll have to excuse our bothering you, boys," said he of the bass voice; "but you see we made a mistake. We're revenue officers, looking for a notorious smuggler named Cranston, who operates around this section. We had positive information that he meant to cross over from Canada in a boat that answered the description of yours to a fraction; and as it's the habit of these smugglers to adopt all sorts of disguises, from honest, hard-working fishermen, to anything else that suits their fancy, we guessed they'd taken to wearing khaki to make us believe they were a party of the militia out for a cruise."

"And so we turned back, and planned this nice little surprise, when we saw that you had come in here," remarked a second man, still chuckling.

"Who are you, anyway, boys?" asked the third, who seemed to have more curiosity than his comrades, though his next words explained the reason for this; "because I've got two sturdy scouts, in my house, and they've become so much brighter lads since they joined the patrol that I want to tell you I'm interested in the movement wherever I run across it. And when I tell them about this blunder of ours I'd like to mention names, you know."

"Why, we belong to the Silver Fox Patrol of Cranford Troop of Boys Scouts," remarked Allan, promptly; "this is our assistant scout-master, Thad Brewster, who happens to be the pilot of the trip because Dr. Philander Hobbs, our real leader, had to hurry back home on business; but we didn't worry a bit when that happened, because, you see, Thad is capable of turning the trick; he knows more in a minute about everything in the woods than Dr. Hobbs could learn in ten years."

"Well, well, tell me about that, will you?" exclaimed the man, with some little excitement; "and which of you might be Allan Hollister—I reckon you're that party right now, youngster; and this stout scout here, surely he must be the Bumpus who got into so many bad holes, and yet always managed to crawl out again? Yes, I'm right about that; and let's see, which one might be Giraffe—no need to ask that, when I look around me. Then there was, another they called Step Hen, didn't they, not to mention Davy Jones, Bob White and Smithy? Oh, I know you all, and I want to shake hands with each and every one of you. Say, won't my kids go crazy when they hear that I've actually met up with that lively bunch of scouts."

"W-w-what's all this mean, mister?" asked Bumpus, actually trembling, not with fear any longer, but actual delight to hear himself mentioned in this familiar way by a stranger.

"Well, I'll have to confess that I've taken such a deep interest in what my boys are doing," continued the revenue officer, "that I even read every book they brought into the house; and that's how I came to know about the doings of the Silver Fox Patrol, and who the eight lads were constituting that branch of the scouts. Give me your hand, Mr. Scout-master; I'm proud to know you, sure I am; and I hope you'll send a written word back home to the two ten-year old twins, who know all about what you fellows have been doing in the Blue Ridge, up in Maine, and even as far away as the Rocky Mountains."

The boys were almost stunned by this remarkable information; but they hastened to accept the hand offered them, and received a hearty squeeze in return.

"My name is Stebbens, and the boys are Daniel and Luther," continued the officer who seemed not quite mind the disappointment of failing to effect an important capture, when the little adventure had give him a story to carry back home to those twins he thought so much of.

"Well all this is mighty interesting, John," said the man with the gruff voice, and who seemed to be the leader of the revenue men; "but we mustn't lose any more time here. The sea is nasty, but our boat can stand it, and we know where tricky Cranston is apt to turn up before morning, not ten miles away; so perhaps we'd better be saying good-night to these lads, and starting out again."

He, as well as the third man, insisted on also shaking hands all around before departing, and with such good will that Bumpus was rubbing his fingers for quite some time afterwards, to get the numb feeling out of the same.

But then no one found any fault; in fact they were thrilled by the knowledge that their exploits had been read by other scouts, who cherished a sort of friendly feeling for the members of the Silver Fox Patrol, just from learning about their adventures in a book or so.

They did not feel at all sleepy after the three revenue men had said good-bye, and vanished in the dark night.

"What's the use pushing out there again, and dropping the mud-hook overboard, when we can tie up so nicely right here?" remarked Step Hen.

"Sure," echoed Giraffe, "and then, in the morning I'll show you I haven't forgotten how to make the finest fire you ever heard tell about. Oh I some pumpkins about that same game, ain't I, Bumpus? You ought to know, because you saw me make one when we was nigh about froze to death up there in Maine, and didn't have a single match along with us."

"Well, anyhow, wait till morning," said Thad, knowing that once the tall scout got started on his favorite hobby, there was no way of stopping him until he had the fever satisfied.

Giraffe had once made up his mind that he could make a fire in the primitive fashion by using a little bow, and a revolving stick. Once this trick is learned and it can usually be accomplished in a minute or two; but most boys find themselves unable to master the feat, and give up in despair after long trying.

The tall scout had persisted even when he met with all manner of discouragements. Sometimes, just when he seemed on the point of success, Bumpus would stumble over him, and end the attempt; then an alarm would be sounded when he had gotten his tinder to smoking; and again he lose out. But in the end he had mastered the secret, and ever afterwards it was one of his proudest accomplishments; so that Giraffe always carried that little bow, and some dry tinder along, whenever he left camp, even though it would have been muck easier to put some matches in his pocket.

57

Of course, as they sat there for a while longer, after the boat had been securely tied up to the shore, the talk was mostly about smugglers.

Each of the boys told all they had ever heard about, such slippery customers; and it added to the interest of the occasion to know that they had just been mistaken for a notorious character, for whom the Government revenue men were on the watch.

"All the same," remarked Bumpus, complacently, "I ain't sorry it happened, because you see, only for their mistake we never'd aheard about them twins, Daniel and Luther Stebbens. I'm glad you wrote out that message for 'em, Thad; and after we get back in Cranford I'm meaning to send 'em my picture. Their daddy said they'd like it the worst kind; and come to think of it, I've got a few showing me astanding with my gun acovering them two bad men as had captured me out in the Big Timber, Davy having snapped the picture off on the spot. Mebbe they'll like that!"

He fell to musing over the lively scenes that had accompanied the adventure covered by this episode; and paid no further attention to the rest of the boys, as they continued to exhaust the subject of the smuggler fraternity.

Finally, all of them admitted that they felt sleepy; and since they no longer had reason to experience anything boarding on alarm, it was decided on the whole not to bother keeping watch.

Already the hour must be near midnight, and they needed sleep, so as to be ready to take up duties of another day when morning broke.

Accordingly, each of them was apportioned a place where he could wedge in and in some way manage to obtain the rest of which he was in such need. Bumpus, being so round, and requiring much more space than any one of the six, was given a chance to roll over in the wider territory close to the doors of the hunting cabin, which were not to be closed, as the boys felt they would need air.

He could sit up, and look around, at any time he happened to be awake; but as Bumpus was usually a sound sleeper, none of them expected that he would avail himself of this privilege until they scrambled over his bundled-up figure at daylight.

In that cove at the mouth of the little creek it was as quiet and peaceful as any heart could wish. Let the wind and the waves hold high carnival outside, nothing gave promise of disturbing the slumber of the tired cruisers.

An hour, two of them and more, crept by, and everything remained as calm as when the scouts folded their blankets about them like Indian warriors, and squeezed in where they had been apportioned.

The clouds had broken, and the moon was shining brightly in the sky overhead when Bumpus, being awakened by some sort of dream, suddenly sat upright, digging his knuckles into his eyes, as if hardly able to believe that he was not safe and sound in his own bed at home.

A nasty snarl struck his ear, and gave him a shock, so that he instantly found himself wide-awake, and looking around to see what had caused the sound.

What he saw must have aroused the fat scout not a little, for immediately his voice was heard in the land, arousing the balance of the sleepers, and doubtless thrilling them through and through.

"Stop thief! Here, let that alone, I tell you! Wake up everybody, and do something, can't you? He's getting away with my lovely trout, I tell you. Hey! Giraffe, ain't you agoing to save your breakfast?"

CHAPTER XII

A CALL TO BREAKFAST

Every one came tumbling out in a great hurry. The moon was so situated that the forepart of the boat was somewhat in the shadow; and on this account they could not see plainly, save that there was some sort of an animal crouching there. As Bumpus had so loudly wailed that it was trying to carry off his prize trout, which had been left hanging in the air until needed at breakfast time, the rest of the boys understood the situation pretty well. Immediately they started to shout, and wave their arms, as well as hurl every sort of thing they could lay hands on.

Naturally enough this proved too much for even the bravest wild beast; and giving a savage snarl the thing suddenly bounded ashore, and was lost to view. They had just a last glimpse of a shadowy figure skulking off along the sandy beach near by.

"Oh! tell me, did he get away with it?" cried Bumpus; and to hear the pain which he threw into these words one would have though a priceless treasure was involved; and so it was, the biggest speckled trout he had ever caught in all his life.

Giraffe scrambled forward, waving his arms in order to discourage any beast that might think to attack him, and "shooing" at a vigorous rate.

"Brace up, Bumpus!" he called out.

"Is it safe?" demanded the fat scout, joyously.

"Yes, he didn't dare carry it off when we got to shouting so lively; and here's your trout, but I reckon we had better take care to make it secure next time. These cats can climb some, and that's right."

"Was it really a wildcat?" asked Step Hen, curiously; just as though the beast had seemed so large to his excited fancy that he would have felt safe in calling it a panther.

"Looked mighty much that way," admitted Allan, who ought to know the breed, as considerable of his younger life had been spent up in the Adirondacks, and in Maine, where he must have seen many a specimen of the feline tribe.

"I thought at first it was a tiger," Bumpus admitted, faintly; at which there was a little laugh all around, for they could easily understand how a fellow's fears might magnify things, when suddenly aroused, and with only that deceptive moonlight to see by.

"Whatever it was, and we'll try and make sure in the morning," remarked

Thad, "it's gone now."

"But it may come back, after smelling of my fine trout," Bumpus observed, seriously; "and rather than run any chance, I think I'll have to sit up, and play sentry the balance of the night."

"Joke!" chuckled Giraffe, chuckling again.

"Huh! mebbe, now, you think I couldn't do that same?" remonstrated Bumpus. "I know I'm a good sound sleeper, which fact I can't deny; but then there's such a thing as rising to an occasion, you see."

"Yes," scoffed the tall scout, "if we depended on you staying awake, chances are we'd have no trout for breakfast to-morrow morning."

"No need of anything like that," remarked the scout-master; "because we can fix it so that no wildcat could get that fish, let him try as hard as he wants. Just you leave it with me, Bumpus, and I'll guarantee that we have fish for breakfast, and without anybody having to stay up either, or lose another minute's sleep."

He tied a cord to the dangling trout, once more placed where it had been before, and then announced that he meant to fasten the other end to his arm. If anything pulled at the fish it would telegraph the fact down to him; and as Thad took the double-barreled shotgun to bed with him, and occupied the place Rumpus had vacated, they understood what the answer was going to be should he be aroused.

But evidently the beast thought discretion the better part of valor, for he did not come aboard again that night. Possibly the shouts, and the whooping of the boys had given him all the excitement he could stand. He liked fish very much; as do all of the cat species, but if he must have a feast of trout it looked as though he would have to procure the same in some other way than stealing it from those on board the Chippeway Belle.

Strange to say Bumpus was the first to crawl out; and his labored progress over his comrades evoked a continual series of grunts and complaints.

"Hurrah! it's still there, and we ain't going to be cheated out of our treat after all!" he was heard to cry, as he gained the open air.

"Well, here's the first case on record of that fellow ever getting awake ahead of the rest of the bunch," said Step Hen.

"Yes, and he mighty near flattened me into a pancake when he crawled on top of me to get to the doors," grunted Giraffe.

"Say, where's my other shoe? Anybody seen my leather around? I bet you now some fellow just grabbed it up, and tossed the same to that pesky old cat last night; and if so, how'm I ever to limp around with only one shoe for my both feet; because some of the things went into the water, for I heard the splash?"

"If anybody threw it, you did yourself, Step Hen," asserted Giraffe, not liking this thing of being accused of things promiscuously; "because I saw something that looked mighty much like a shoe, in your hand when you crawled out."

"Then why didn't, you tell me about it, Giraffe?" complained the other, with a doleful groan. "I think you're about as mean as you can be, to let a poor fellow in his excitement do such a thing."

"Why, however was I to know?" said the tall scout, chuckling as though it struck him as a joke that Step Hen, in his sudden anxiety to scare the prowler away, should have thrown his own shoe at the cat. "Besides, I had troubles of my own, just about that time, let me tell you. But mebbe you can find your old shoe again; because the water ain't so very deep up ahead there."

"No need to bother," sang out Bumpus, who was taking his trout down tenderly, and examining it to see how much damage the claws of the intruder had done, if any, "because there the shoe is right now, on shore, and all right."

That gave Step Hen reason to say he knew he could never have been silly enough to cast his shoe in such a way as to hurl it overboard; but all the same he was pleased to be able to recover it in a dry condition, after all.

"Who'll clean it while I get a fire started ashore?" asked Giraffe, presently, when they had finished their dressing.

"No hurry," remarked Thad; "for while the sun's getting ready to come up, and the storm petered out after all, I guess the lake's a bit too rough for us to go out for some time yet. Such a big body of water can kick up some sea when it gets in the humor; and some of the party don't seem to hanker after that rising and falling motion."

Bumpus himself decided to do the last honors to his "noble capture," and taking the fish ashore, with a hunting knife that had a keen edge, he looked for a good place to sit down, on a rock bordering the little beach. Here he kept industriously at work for quite some time.

Meanwhile the fire was a big success, for Giraffe certainly was a marvel when it came to knowing all there was about making them. He had found just the finest hole to serve as the bed of his cooking fire, where a body of red embers would after a little while invite them to place their frying-pan and coffee-pot on the iron grating they carried for the purpose, and which was really the gridiron-like contrivance belonging to a cast-off stove's oven.

"I say, Thad!" Bumpus was heard calling, after he had had plenty of time to finish his job with the trout.

"What do you want now, Bumpus?" replied the scout-master, cheerily.

"Come down here, won't you, and settle something for me."

So Thad hastened to accommodate him; and several of the other fellows followed at his heels, being consumed by curiosity, perhaps; or it might be they suspected something of the truth, and wished to hear Thad's decision in the matter.

"Now what?" asked the scout-master, as he reached the spot.

"I wish you'd tell me what sort of a critter that was last night," Bumpus remarked, as he pointed down near his feet; "because he ran along here when he skedaddled off; and you can see the prints as plain as anything."

"I should say it was a wildcat; but let's ask Allan, to make sure," replied the patrol leader, and upon reaching the spot, Allan instantly declared the same thing.

At that Bumpus appeared to be satisfied; and as the trout was now ready for the pan they adjourned to where the fire was waiting, with a hungry looking cook in readiness to get things going.

Just as they anticipated, that trout was elegant—no other word Bumpus could conjure up would begin to do justice to the feast they had that morning. And the proud captor of the prize cast many a look in the direction of his rival, which of course the envious Giraffe construed to mean; "see what I can do when I set my mind on a job; and get busy yourself."

But then Giraffe had just had a pretty generous second portion of the salmon-colored fish steak, and was in no humor to get huffy.

He did start in right after breakfast to get several lines out, and attended to the same assiduously all morning. Between the busy workers they managed to pull in five fish, of which Bumpus took two. So that thus far the score was even, as regards numbers, though the fat scout was still "high notch" when the question of size was concerned.

"I see that before we get back home we'll all have swelled heads," Thad remarked, with a broad, smile; and upon the others demanding to know what he meant, he went on to say: "why, don't you know, scientists unite in declaring that fish is the greatest brain food going; so if these fellows keep on loading us down with trout and white fish and every other kind that lives in this big lake, why, our hats will soon be too small for our enlarged craniums."

"Oh! we can afford to take the chances of that!" laughed Allan.

As the wind had gone down, and the waves with it to a considerable extent, it was decided that they might make a start after an early lunch. Thad consulted his Government Survey charts, and marked a place that he believed would make them a good harbor, and which they ought to reach with any reasonable luck.

This being settled they got underway about half-past eleven; and when the little cruiser left the shelter of the cove, and once more breasted the rising and falling waves, Bumpus shook his head dismally, and loudly hoped he would not once more have to spend all his time feeding the fishes. But his fears proved groundless, for they had apparently become used to the motion of the waves, and not one of them became seasick again that day.

CHAPTER XIII

UP AGAINST IT AGAIN

"Everything is lovely, and the goose hangs high! This makes the fifth day since we started out; and things seem to be going along right smoothly at the old stand, don't they, fellows?"

Giraffe asked this question. He was lying on his back on top of the hunting-cabin of the little cruiser, taking what he termed a "sun bath;" but which some of his chums always called "being too lazy too move."

"And so far none of us have felt the least bit seasick again," remarked Step Hen, with what sounded like a fervent note of thanksgiving in his voice, as though of all the mean things he could imagine, that of feeling a sinking sensation at the pit of the stomach excelled.

"And I'm still leading Giraffe by three fish," declared Bumpus; "besides having caught the biggest fish and the longest one in the bargain. Better wake up, and get a move on you, Giraffe, or be counting on doing all the drudgery when we have that blow-out supper on our return home."

"I ain't worrying any, Bumpus," lazily returned the other; "fact is, it tickles me just to see you hustle around in your great fishing stunt. Sure you're getting peaked, and as thin as anything, after such unusual exertions. I wouldn't be surprised if some show offered you a job as the Living Skeleton, if this thing keeps up much longer, because you're fading away right along."

Bumpus looked himself all over, and if there was a shade of anxiety on his rosy face it did not stay there long.

"I only wished what you said was half-way true, Giraffe," he sighed; "but seems like nothing is ever agoing to take off two pounds from my weight. I can't honestly see where there's a mite of a change; and I know you can't neither. Stop your kidding, and get your lines out again. I had a sure-enough nibble right then, and if you don't look out, I'll be pulling in a dandy fish."

"Wake me up when you do, and I'll start in. You get 'em worked-up like, and then I'll show you how to do the trick. Up to now I've just been playing possum, you know, but look out whenever I do get going."

"Bah! who's afraid?" scoffed the fat scout, finding a use for his favorite expression, to show his contempt for the threat of Giraffe.

"But we've gone over a heap of ground during the five days we've been afloat on this inland sea, haven't we, boys?" remarked Step Hen.

"I'd like to, know why you call it ground, when, we've been moving over water all the time?" observed Davy, who was not as happy as most of his chums, because this way of living offered him no chance to climb trees, and hang from limbs, as was his favorite habit; and therefore time hung heavy on his hands, so that he grew restless.

"Oh! well, it doesn't make any difference that I can see," replied Step Hen; "a rose by any other name would smell as sweet, they say. But we have covered a heap of distance, you'll admit, Davy."

"Yes, and had lots of fun in the bargain," Allan put in.

"Thanks to the weather man for keeping things nice for us, and not allowing any storm along," suggested Bumpus.

"Well, you may have reason to change your tune soon, old fellow," warned

Giraffe with an ominous shake of his head.

"Now, what makes you go and say that, Giraffe? Do you know anything, or are you just trying to bother me on general principles?" demanded the stout boy, aggressively.

"Well, perhaps you didn't know it," remarked the other, carelessly, "but latterly I've taken a notion to study to become a weather prophet. On the sly I've been getting all the information about goose bones, and all sorts of signs, wherever I could strike the same. Then I've studied up how the fellows down at Washington make their guesses, and I'm getting there right smart. Why, every morning now, for the last three days I've told myself it was agoing to be fair, and she was, sure pop. Understand that, Bumpus?"

"I thought something was bothering you, and keeping you from getting as many fish as I did; but what about this morning, Giraffe, did it look any different to you; and is the good weather acoming to an end?" asked Bumpus.

"The signs all pointed to a change this morning," replied the other. "Now, don't expect me to go into particulars, because there ain't any need of more'n one weather sharp in our crowd. And say, just cast your eye over there to the southwest; don't you see that low bank of clouds along the horizon? Well, when they get to moving up on us, we're bound to have, high winds, and p'raps a regular howler of a storm."

Bumpus' face assumed a serious look as he turned quickly to the scout-master.

"What do you say, Thad?" he queried, for it was never possible to know whether Giraffe were working off one of his little practical jokes or not, he had such a way of looking very solemn, even while chuckling inwardly.

"I don't count much on his knowledge of telling in the morning what sort of a day it's going to be," replied the other, with a shake of the head; "but what he says about those clouds is as near facts as Giraffe ever gets."

"Then there is a storm bound to swoop down on us?" demanded Bumpus, as he cast a nervous glance around at the watery expanse; for they were far out on the lake.

"I'm afraid we'll have a rough night of it," Thad confessed; "but if we're only safe in a harbor by evening, we won't need to bother our heads any about that."

"Then we won't have any trouble about making that safe harbor, will we?" continued Bumpus, who could be very positive and persistent whenever he wanted to know anything, so that it was a difficult thing to shunt him aside.

"If the engine holds out we ought to be there by five, I expect," Thad answered.

Bumpus transferred his attention to the working motor; and his look of anxiety increased.

"Seems to me you've been pottering more'n a little with that thing today,

Thad," he went on to say.

"Yes, and right now it don't work decent," observed Step Hen. "It misses an explosion every third one, and acts like it might go out of business any minute on us, that's right, fellows."

Some of the rest began to look sober at this. Giraffe, who had thought to have a joke at the expense of his plump rival, no longer lay there, sprawled upon the roof of the hunting cabin of the launch; but sat up to observe the singular actions of the engine for himself. Nor did he, appear to get much consolation from what he discovered.

"I declare now if it ain't a fact, boys," he said, seriously. "She acts mighty like she wanted to throw up the sponge, and let us hustle to get ashore the best way we could. Of all the contrary things commend me to a balky engine on a cruiser. And Dr. Hobbs was thinkin' his friend was doing us the greatest favor going to loan him this old trap, that like's not he keeps heavily insured, in the hopes that some fine day she'll go down, when he can buy a newer and better, model with the money he collects."

"Oh! I wouldn't say that, if I were you, Giraffe,'" remarked Thad. "From the way the gentleman wrote to Dr. Hobbs I'm sure he thought he was doing us a favor; and you know it's bad manners to look a gift horse in the mouth. If he was charging us a round sum for the use of the boat we, might say something; but outside of the gasoline we consume we don't have to put out a cent."

"But do you really expect the rickety old engine'll go back on us before we get to that harbor you're heading for?" demanded Bumpus.

"How can I tell?" Thad replied. "I'm doing everything I know of to coax it to be good. If anybody has a scheme for helping along, the rest of us would be glad to listen to the same, and take it up too, if there was a ghost of a show that we could profit by doing that."

Apparently nobody did have any idea of bettering conditions as they now prevailed; for not a word came in reply, to Thad's request for several minutes. During this time the boys sat there and watched the queer actions of the engine that Thad was bending over, now doing this and again that in order to see whether he could not obtain more profitable results from the laboring motor.

"I s'pose now," Bumpus finally did muster up courage enough to say, "if it came to the worst, and you saw we couldn't make that harbor, why, you might head her on to the beach, so that we could get ashore, no matter what, happened to the old ship?"

"Yes, how about that, Thad?" questioned Step Hen, as though somehow a thought along the same lines might have been passing through his mind just then.

Thad shook his head in the negative.

"That would be a risky proceeding, at any time," he observed, "when you consider that the shore along here is composed of sharp-pointed rocks, and that if there was any sea on at all we'd probably be wrecked long before we could land. That must mean we'd all be thrown into the surf, and perhaps lose our lives trying to swim ashore among the rocks. No we'll have to try some other plan than that, or else stick to the boat, and hope the storm won't be so very bad after all."

"Well, one thing sure," said Davy Jones, who had not taken any part in this conversation thus far, "the clouds are coming along right speedy. Since I first took note they've crept up till they look twice as big now."

This news was not pleasant for them to hear, though every one realized that the speaker was not "drawing the long bow" when he made the assertion.

Yes, they could almost note the rising of the dark mass. If it kept on as it was doing, inside of half an hour the heavens would be obscured above, and perhaps the forerunner of the gale be upon them.

Bumpus quickly started to pulling in the various fish lines he had been trailing along after the boat, in hopes of meeting up with a hungry fish that might be taken aboard, and not only afford a meal for the crowd, but give him a good chance to crow over his rival fisherman once more, "rub it in," as he called it.

Thad got out his charts, and the whole lot bent over, while he pointed out where they were just then, and the distant harbor he had hoped to reach.

"If it comes to the worst," ventured Allan, "there's that lone island ahead of us, Sturgeon Island it's called on the chart, and we might get in the lee of that."

CHAPTER XIV

THE SQUALL

"Sturgeon Island, did you say, Allan?" remarked Step Hen. "Sounds like it might be a good fishing place. If we happened to land there, perhaps Bumpus and Giraffe might manage to do some big stunts, pulling in sturgeon. Can anybody tell me what sort of a fish that is, anyway? I never saw one, or a fellow that caught one, either."

"Oh! they grow to big size, and are caught in the Great Lakes in this country. They take sturgeon eggs I believe to make this high-priced stuff they use in the tony clubs and call caviar, or something like that," observed Bumpus, who really did know considerable about fish and fishing, though of course he did not claim to be a fly fisherman, capable of casting seventy feet or more.

But the subject did not interest any of them just then. The way that bank of ominous clouds kept advancing higher and higher soon kept their attention riveted in that quarter.

"About how far away from our harbor are we, Thad?" asked Step Hen.

"Something like fifteen miles, I should say," came the reply.

Giraffe looked at the balky engine, and shook his head.

"Then we'd better make up our minds right here and now that we'll never get to that place this day," he said, positively; and there was no one bold enough to accept of the plain challenge his tones conveyed.

"That means our only hope lies in Sturgeon Island, don't it?" Bumpus asked.

"Looks that way," Thad told him.

"But that don't seem so far on the map; you, just put your finger on the same, Thad; and if she's close enough to do that, hadn't we ought to see that island, ahead somewhere?"

"Suppose you take the glasses and look," suggested the pilot, who was busy with the engine that had stopped short again, and needed coaxing to take up its burden once more, "It's rather hazy, you'll notice, so that you couldn't be sure of anything more than three miles away, I reckon; but tell us what lies de ahead, will you, Bumpus?"

A minute later, and the fat scout cried out in considerable excitement:

"I can see land ahead, sure I can, fellows!"

"That must be the island, then," rejoined Thad, busily engaged.

"Our only hope, so we had ought to call it our island," Davy went on to say, as he deliberately took the glasses from Bumpus, and glued the smaller end of the same to his own eyes.

Then in turn everybody but Thad had to have a chance to look; and in the end it was the consensus of opinion that Bumpus had spoken only the truth when he said there were positive evidences of some sort of land ahead.

"Oh! if you could only get that old junk-shop engine to working for half an hour, Thad, we'd have plenty of time to circle around to the leeward side of that island, and then we could get ashore, no matter what happened to the Belle," Bumpus faltered, as he watched the skipper still working as rapidly as he could.

All at once the machinery started up again, when Thad gave the crank a whirl.

"Bully for you, Thad!" cried Davy, slapping the other heartily on the back; and then turning to look at the black clouds following after them, as though he would give fair warning that they meant to make a stiff fight for the opportunity of finding safety.

"Go slow!" warned the other; "don't be too sure, because she's limping already, and I'd hate to risk my reputation in saying that we could depend on that thing five minutes at a stretch," and from the way Thad said this it was evident that he had by now almost lost all faith in the motor.

"Looks like it might be a race between the storm, and our getting behind Sturgeon Island," said Giraffe, as he turned alternately from stem to stern of the boat, evidently trying to figure out what sort of chance they might have for winning out in the end.

But they knew that it all depended on the engine; if it worked as well as it was doing right now they could surely pass over the few miles that separated them from the island; and once in its lee it would not be so difficult to gain the shore. Neither the wild wind, nor the gathering waves could disturb them, so long as the storm continued to come out of the south-west, for they were now cruising along the northern shore of the great lake, where the Dominion of Canada held sway, and not Uncle Sam.

So they watched it anxiously, and every time it missed an explosion Bumpus would utter a grunt or a groan; only to catch new inspiration and hope when he found that it was a false alarm, and that they were still going right along.

Thad was doing everything he knew how to encourage the engine to keep up the good work; but he had already made up his mind to be surprised at nothing. There was a possibility that it might keep working fairly well as long as they wanted, in order to find safety in the shelter of the island; and then again it was apt to let down at any minute.

Thad, however, was not the one to show the white feather. He knew that there were several of his chums who might not be constituted just the same as he and Allan, and Giraffe—Bumpus and Davy and Step Hen; and his seeming cheerfulness was partly assumed in order to buoy their drooping spirits up; as scout-master Thad felt that he had many duties to perform, and one of these was to instill a feeling of confidence in the breasts of his comrades.

"I can see a white streak on the water away back there!" announced

Giraffe, presently.

"That's where you've got the advantage of the rest of us, with your long neck, and that way of stretching the same," complained Step Hen; and determined to meet the other on his own grounds he clambered to the top of the cabin, where he could use the glasses he had taken from the hand of Giraffe.

"It's the first blow of the squall, as sure as anything," he immediately reported; which news made Bumpus turn pale; for he had not forgotten what he experienced on that other occasion.

"Coming racing after us, like hot cakes!" added Giraffe. "Hadn't we better get them life preservers out, and fastened on under our arms, Thad? Then, if so be the old tub did take a notion to turn turtle, we'd have some show for our money."

"Make him stop talking that way, Thad, won't you?" urged Bumpus; "he just does it to make me have a bad feeling down here," and he rubbed his projecting stomach mournfully as he spoke.

"No, I'm sorry to tell you he isn't saying anything too strong, Bumpus," the skipper of the Chippeway Belle assured him; and after that poor Bumpus had nothing more to say; only he clutched the cork and canvas life preserver which was handed out to him, and with trembling hands proceeded to adjust the same under his arms; though it was a very snug fit, even if Giraffe had given him the largest in the lot under the seats.

"If anything happens, remember," said Thad, in all seriousness, as he watched the rapid way in which that ominous white line on the water was racing after them; "all of you try your best to land on the island. We're getting closer all the while to the same, and there seems to be some shore for us to crawl up, because, with the rocks I can see little patches of gravelly beach. Keep your eyes fixed on that, and do everything you can to get there in case of a wreck."

"Wreck!" muttered Bumpus, as though talking to himself, as he often did when in trouble. "Didn't I dream I was on a ship that went to pieces in storm; and first thing I knew I had to swim for it, and me knowing so little about doing that. Oh! I hope nothing happens, and that we ran swing around back of that bully old island soon!"

"So say we all of us, Bumpus," Giraffe echoed; and he did not mean to draw the attention of the others to the shaky condition of the fat scout, because, if the truth were told, every one of the six boys would be found to be quivering with the dreadful suspense, while waiting for that forerunner of the squall to strike them.

The engine still continued to keep them moving, although to the excited imagination of some of the boys they seemed to be almost standing still.

"What do you think of it now, Thad?" asked Step Hen, with the manner of one who hoped for good tidings, yet feared the worst.

"I don't just like the looks of that first rush of wind," replied the pilot; "of course if we pull through that we may be able to hold out, and gradually force a way around the island. I'm trying to head as near as I dare, because if once we're forced past, there's nothing left for us, you understand?"

Yes, they could grasp that point well enough, and Step Hen even besought the one at the wheel to work in a little closer.

"Better take the chances of being thrown on the island than to be carried past by a fluke of the wind!" he declared, and Thad believed so much the same way that he did change their course slightly.

The boys had brought out what most they wanted to save in case of a wreck. One carried his clothes bag, with the blanket fastened to the same; another had the double-barreled shotgun; while Giraffe made sure to see that his fishing tackle was safely tucked in with his belongings, which he had made up into as small a compass as possible.

As for Bumpus, he had gathered everything he owned, and looked as though he might be a walking peddler trying to dispose of his wares to the country people. On the other hand there was Step Hen who did not appear to care an atom about his clothes and his blanket; but he had managed to wrap something around the owl, and was all the while gripping the bird tightly; though Bumpus said he was silly to risk his own life, when all he had to do was to cut the cord he had put around the cloth, unfasten the chain that gripped the bird's leg, and give him a toss into the air, when Jim would look out for himself.

"Wish I could fly away as easy as he can," Bumpus wound up with; but in spite of all these suggestions the obstinate Step Hen still persisted in holding on to his prisoner, as though he meant to accept every chance rather than let him go.

"Hold fast, everybody, for here she comes!" called Allan, presently.

The puttering of the escape connection with the engine could no longer be heard, because of the roar made by the rushing wind, and the splash of the curling water, as the squall leaped forward and rapidly overtook them.

"Oh; my stars!" Bumpus was heard to call out, as he clung to something with all his might and main; for the little cruiser seemed to be lifted high in the air, and carried forward on the top of a giant billow, only to sink down in the trough of the sea with a heavy motion; but still keeping head on.

But in that moment of time Thad Brewster knew that the fate of the boat was effectually sealed; because the engine had given its last throb and they were now a helpless, drifting object in the midst of those angry waters!

CHAPTER XV

CLEVER WORK

Imagine the horror of the six scouts when they realized that they were now completely at the mercy of the storm, since the last barrier seemed to have given way when the treacherous engine broke down.

Even brave-hearted Thad Brewster felt that their case was desperate: and he knew in his secret heart that if they managed to escape a serious situation it must be through a narrow gap.

At the same time Thad always made it a point to put on a good face when up against trouble. This was of course partly done because of his comrades, since, as the scout-master he felt more responsibility than fell to the share of the rest.

Bumpus had been hanging on like a good fellow. He greatly feared lest some sudden violent lurch of the boat toss him headlong into that yeasty sea; which he was gazing upon with terror.

At the same time Bumpus had been closely observing the actions of the eccentric motor, and was one of the first to discover that it had petered out, giving up the ghost completely, as Giraffe would have said.

"Oh! what can we do now, Thad?" shouted the stout scout, as usual turning to the quick-witted one in an emergency; but for once even Thad was at his wit's ends to know what to attempt, the situation was that desperate.

"Everybody hold on!" was all Thad called back.

There was hardly any need of this injunction, for each fellow had managed to brace himself, so that unless the boat actually "turned turtle," or at least was thrown on her beam ends, they could not be dislodged.

Thad was straining his eyesight as best he could, endeavoring to see ahead. The furious wind of course made this a difficult task, because it not only sent the waves high, but as these broke into foam along their crests, this was actually cut off as with an invisible knife, and blown away in the shape of flying spud; so that the very air was surcharged with a fine mist, rendering it hard to distinguish anything fifty feet off.

Of course it was the island that the young leader was striving to see all this while. He knew as well as anything that the one slim hope remaining to them must rest upon their chance of finding some sort of shelter behind this oasis in the watery waste.

At one time it had been Thad's hope that if the worst came they might find themselves thrown on the windward side of Sturgeon Island. Now he knew that this had been rendered an utter impossibility; because the storm had swept down upon them so rapidly after their course was changed that there had been no time for the cruiser to reach a position that would bring about any such result.

And then besides, the surf must be dashing high over that exposed end of the rocky island, so that even though they struck, it might be on an outer reef. In such a case who could say whether any of the boys would manage to overcome the terrible difficulties lying in wait, and be thrown up on a sandy beach, rather than dashed ruthlessly against the cruel rocks?

So Thad crouched there near the bow, holding on desperately, and hoping for he hardly knew what, save that he seemed to have an inspiration there presently would come a slender chance for them to survive the blow.

"There's the island!" yelled Giraffe, pointing to the right.

Thad had seen it before the other thus called attention to the fact of their being so near safety, yet unable to quite reach it.

"But we're going along past it!" shrieked Bumpus. "Thad, ain't there any way we could work in? Oh! think quick, please, or, it'll be too late!"

They were moving quite fast, with wind and wave joining forces to sweep the little helpless craft along. Just as Bumpus had said, unless something could be done immediately it must surely be too late; for once they left the island behind, the whole immense inland sea would be before them; and their hopes of surviving the storm must sink too close upon the zero mark.

Thad was thinking as fast as he could; indeed, his very brain seemed to be on fire, such was the mental energy he was expending. But really there was nothing in the wide world that could be done then.

True, they had push-poles, but doubtless the depth of water would have rendered these utterly useless, even had they started to handle them. Nothing was to be hoped for in the direction of the engine, since that had collapsed in the most cowardly fashion at the first swoop of the blow.

What then?

Thad had made one little discovery that gave a slender promise of succor; and it is strange upon what a small foundation hopes can be built at such a time as this. He saw that the wind had shifted just a little; but this was enough to carry the drifting launch a trifle toward the side of the island.

Now, it did not stand to reason that they would strike, no matter how long that shore turned out to be; because there was enough current to sheer them off; but when the lower end of the island was reached, Thad really believed there might be a sudden inward sweep of the water that had been so long held at bay by the rocky shore.

There always is more or less of this eddy at the end of an island in a river; and upon a large lake in our country it may be found as a rule toward the eastern terminus, since the prevailing storms come from the west, southwest and northwest.

The only question with the anxious lad was whether this eddy would have sufficient "pull" to drag them in behind the island. Upon that one small possibility rested all their hopes.

Thad knew that possibly he and his chums might render some assistance at this critical moment, if so be they were ready.

"Allan—Giraffe, come here!" he called out.

The two scouts heard him above all the racket of the elements, which, what with the howling of the wind, the breaking of the waves against the boat, and the roar of the surf on the exposed end of the island, amounted to a tremendous volume of sound.

"Ay! ay!" Giraffe was heard to cry in return, as he proceeded to make his way forward, clinging to every object that offered a stable hold, because the wind seemed trying its level best to tear him away.

Bumpus also heard the call, but as his name had not been mentioned he dared not take it upon himself to move so much as one of his tightly braced feet. He seemed to feel that if he did so it would be at the risk of his life; and the thought of being cast adrift on that raging sea filled him with actual terror.

Could those boys have had a vivid picture of that scene just then, they would never have been able to look at it again without shivering; because their faces must certainly have expressed the sensations that filled their hearts to overflowing.

But Davy, as the official photographer of the patrol, was too much concerned just then in holding on, to dream of making any use of his vest pocket kodak; nor would it have been possible to have obtained any sort of view under such stormy conditions as surrounded them.

"What is it, Thad?"

Giraffe asked this question as he and the other scout managed to come close to where the patrol leader clung.

"We've got a little chance when we get to the end of the island, don't you see?" Thad bawled, making use of one hand to serve in lieu of a speaking trumpet. "We're getting closer all the time, and will just skim past the last rock. And then is our chance, when we strike the eddy there always is beyond an island. Do you understand?"

Both scouts nodded their heads violently, and Giraffe called out:

"What d'ye want us to do, Thad?"

"We must get the setting poles out, and be ready to try and push with all our might and main when the time comes. Everything depends on that!" Thad replied, also, at the top of his strong, young voice.

"But it may be too deep!" objected Giraffe; though at the same time fumbling with the rope that fastened one of the push-poles in question to the deck alongside the cabin roof.

"We've got to take the chances of that," Thad went on; "and besides, you know it always shallows where the sand is washed around the point of an island. Hurry, fellows, because we must be nearly there!"

He lent a hand himself, for he saw that Giraffe was meeting with more or less difficulty in releasing the pole toward which he had turned his attention; though had the conditions been different, the boy might not have had the slightest trouble about getting it free. The boat was pitching so furiously, that he could only use one hand, because it was necessary for him to grasp some hold, lest he be tossed overboard, as a bucking bronco hurls an unsuspecting rider from the saddle by a quick upward movement.

Hardly had they secured possession of the two long and stout poles than the end of the island hove in sight. They were very close to it now; indeed, it almost seemed as though an agile fellow might have made a flying leap, and with half-way decent luck manage to alight on the sentinel rock that guarded this point.

But no one tried that desperate game; in fact, it was doubtful whether it even occurred to Davy or Step Hen before they had been carried past, and the widening gulf rendered such a movement impossible of accomplishment.

But the three lads toward the bow of the drifting boat were desperately engaged in trying to swerve the cruiser more and more behind the island, ere they got so far that they would lose the benefits of the half-way calm condition existing in the lee of the shore.

Fortunately the water did prove to be fairly shallow at this point, just as the scout-master had predicted; for vast quantities of sand had been deposited there from time to time through such storms as the present one, and also the melting of the ice that drifted there during each breaking-up season for ages past.

The poles easily reached bottom and secured a firm hold there, so that the boys were enabled to throw their full strength upon the other ends. And the Chippeway Bell was thus shoved around, so that the anchor, which was watched by Step Hen and Davy Jones, could be easily thrown ahead, thus preventing their drifting further away from the friendly shore. And this having been accomplished the three scouts were almost ready to drop down with fatigue, for they had worked strenuously.

CHAPTER XVI

MAROONED

"Hurrrah!" shouted Bumpus, who had been so worked up during this struggle between his comrades and the greed of the elements, that he had hardly taken time to breathe.

Davy, and Step Hen too, seemed ready to throw up their hats, and cheer with exultation because of their wonderful deliverance from continued perils.

All of them were pretty well soaked, though it had not rained at all; so that their bedraggled condition must have come from the water that was in the air, and an occasional wave that slapped over the boat when it broke.

Although they had apparently secured a firm grip on an anchorage, and it would seem as though their present troubles were over, Thad did not sink down like his two fellow laborers, to pant, and rest up.

He proceeded to scramble aft, for he had made an alarming discovery, and wished to start an investigation at once.

The boat sat much lower in the water than he had ever known it to do; and this circumstance seemed alarming. One look into the cabin told him the reason, nor was Thad very much surprised to find that it was already knee deep in water.

"How did this come in here, fellows?" he asked Davy and Step Hen, who from their positions might be expected to know; "did you notice many waves pour over the stern of the boat?"

"N-no, hardly any water at all came in, Thad," replied Step Hen, astonished when he came to look into the partly submerged cabin for himself.

"She kept riding like a duck, and was ahead of the waves most all the time," was the testimony Davy added; which might be set down as the first words of praise given to the little craft thus far during the cruise.

"Why, goodness gracious, Thad, we must be sinking!" bellowed the amazed Bumpus, also craning his fat neck the best way he could, in order to peer into the cabin.

"Just what she is doing," replied the scoutmaster, composedly; because they were now in comparatively shallow water, out of the reach of the storm; and it did not matter so much what happened after this.

"Sprung a leak, mebbe?" suggested Giraffe, joining the group.

"Wouldn't be surprised if that was what happened," Allan added, as, he too took a survey of the flooded interior.

"Then, like as not she'll go down right under us, after a bit, Thad!" exclaimed Bumpus, in new excitement, as he contemplated the distance still separating them from the point of the island, and mentally figured whether he could float to safety with that life preserver on, and one of his chums towing him.

"She will, and that's a dead sure thing," Giraffe told him.

"We ought to get her in closer before that happens, hadn't, we, fellows?" Step Hen wanted to know.

"We've got to try that same, and right away!" declared Thad, as he stooped to once more; pick up a push-pole.

"Here, you Step, Hen and Davy, take hold in our place, because you're fresh, and ought to do better work," Giraffe remarked, as he thrust his pole into the hands of the former.

Now, under ordinary conditions Step Hen might have wanted to know by what authority the lengthy, scout presumed to order him around, when they were of the same rank in the patrol; but he realized the force of what Giraffe had said, and hence accepted the pole without a murmur, starting to work immediately; while, Davy did the same with the one Thad allowed him to take.

"When you get the boat part way up toward where the anchor holds," observed the scout-master, "we'll drag the mudhook in, and stand ready to throw it out again. By pulling on the cable after the anchor gets a firm hold on bottom, it's possible to claw the boat along foot by foot. I've done that same many a time; and it'll help out more than a little."

They speedily found that Thad spoke truly, and under the influence of poles as well as the anchor drag the Chippeway Belle began to approach the shore, much to the delight of Bumpus. When the fat scout, closely observing the setting poles as they were dipped repeatedly into the water, discovered that they struck bottom in a depth of not more than four feet, he was ready to shout with joy. That meant it could not be over his head; and if the worst came, he might wade to land.

Despite the fact that their vessel was a wreck, and about to sink, the boys had no desire to complain just then. Their escape from threatening danger had been too recent for them to feel ungrateful. Later on the grumblers would no doubt start to work in their customary way, and find cause for venting their disgust because things did not come out as they might have wished; but even Giraffe was bubbling over with satisfaction when he realized that they had actually managed to cheat the storm after all.

It had been a close shave, however, and only for that bright thought on the part of Thad, they might at that very moment have been drifting far away, with their boat slowly but purely sinking, despite all the baling they could accomplish.

But then, what was the good of scout-masters if they were not able to do the thinking for the crowd, the reckless Giraffe would possibly have said, if the question had been put up to him.

Everybody was working like the busy bees; even Bumpus tried to assist in hauling at the cable, having moved forward when the boat no longer pranced and bobbed on the agitated sea like a skittish horse.

Of course, as the water was coming in so fast, the cruiser was bound to presently strike bottom; but it was the design of Thad to work her in just as far as possible, for as they had a block and tackle aboard he hoped they would be able to make some sort of rude "ways," where she might be hauled out later on, patched up, and their interrupted cruise continued.

"Stuck fast, Thad; she's on bottom, and no use straining to try and get her another inch toward the shore!" announced Allan, presently; and all of them realized that he spoke the absolute truth when he said this.

"Well," remarked Bumpus, complacently, "we are on the wreck of our noble ship, and close enough to shore to salvage all our possessions; which I consider the greatest of good luck. Who'll carry me on his shoulders, now?"

Strange to say, nobody offered to undertake this task, where Bumpus pretended to feel very much hurt, though in reality quite merry.

"I was afraid you'd all speak at once, and have a quarrel over the honor; but looks now like I might have to do the grand wading act myself, holding up my clothes-bag and blanket, to keep from getting the same more soaked than they are now. If we could only make a raft like old Robinson Crusoe did, it would be fine. Can we get this cabin roof off, and would it float, do you think, Thad?"

"We'll wade!" replied the scout-master, grimly, and that settled it.

"The sooner the better," remarked Giraffe, "because night's going to drop down on us right early to-day, and we ought to have a warm fire started somehow, so's to dry us off," for Giraffe had the utmost faith in a fire being able to do about nearly everything necessary to the good cheer of mankind, because he fairly worshipped a jolly blaze.

Indeed, as most of them had commenced to shiver already, owing to their wet condition, and the stress of excitement under which they had been recently laboring, the thought of sitting before a comfortable fire did seem to buoy up their spirits amazingly.

"Get ready to slip over, and go ashore!" ordered Thad, "I'll take the anchor cable with me, and see that it's made fast to a rock or a tree. We may find a chance to mend the boat, and anyway it's just as well that we try and keep her here; though if the wind whips around no cable would hold her, I reckon."

Giraffe was the first to drop over. The water hardly came above his waist; but then his height was responsible for this, and cautious Bumpus did not deceive himself on that account. Still he found that he could easily wade, and in a short time all of them had reached the friendly rocks.

Here Thad made the rope secure.

"I'm going back for a few more things, and you might come along with me,

Allan," the scout-master remarked.

"I reckon you think there's a pretty good possibility that the wind will veer around, sooner or later, and that the old tub won't be in sight when morning comes?" Allan remarked, as he pushed out alongside his chum.

"Chances tend that way," was the replied Thad, "and anyhow, it's better that we get all the supplies we have ashore. Then if 'we have to play Crusoe for a while we'll have something to go on with."

"Our stock happens to be pretty low," remarked Allan; "and Giraffe was only this morning complaining that he didn't get enough to eat, and that we'd better stop off somewhere to buy more bacon and bread and such things. Too bad we didn't think of that when near Duluth, which place you wanted to avoid because of certain reasons."

They made the trip without accident. Then it was considered that about all had been taken from the stranded and half sunken cruiser that was worth salving.

Already was Giraffe hunting for some good place where they might find shelter, and start a fire; for while it had not rained as yet, strange to say, a flood was likely to come down at any moment, so long as the heavens remained as dark as they were still.

Bumpus was looking all around him. He did not wander away from the rest, because it seemed as though that mysterious island on which they had been cast might be inhabited by wild beasts of prey, for all they knew, ready to spring upon a nice, juicy morsel like him, and make a meal. That was one of the disadvantages in being plump, Bumpus always insisted, because envious eyes were won't to fall upon him first of all.

About that time Giraffe hove in sight again, and from his happy manner it was evident that he had important news to communicate.

"Just shoulder your packs, fellows, and come with me," he hastened to tell them. "I've run across the boss place for us to keep under shelter; and there's aplenty of nice dry wood handy, so we can lay in a supply before it rains. After all it strikes me that with our troubles we ought to be thankful things ain't worse'n they are. With a fire a fellow can do nigh anything to make you feel good. Come on!"

CHAPTER XVII

ROBINSON CRUSOE, JR.

"There you are," said Giraffe, presently.

"Why, that shelf of rock looks just like it was meant to keep the rain off," declared Step Hen, delighted at the prospect.

"Hold on," Bumpus advised.

"What ails you now?" Giraffe wanted to know.

"Why, you see," the stout boy went on to say, "she looks kinder dark and gloomy under that same rock."

"But it won't after I get a fire started; you see the night's beginning to settle down already," Giraffe told him.

"How d'ye know there ain't somethin' ahiding in there?" demanded Bumpus.

At that the lengthy scout laughed scornfully. "Oh! that's the way the wind blows, does it? Well, you watch me eat your old wolf up. I'm hungry enough right now to eat anything, I reckon."

Few of them could remember when Giraffe was anything but starving, for he always had that appetite of his along, and working overtime.

He immediately crawled under the ledge, for the shelf of rock was not high enough to admit of his standing erect.

"Seems to be all right," admitted Bumpus.

"Of course it is, though I kind o' think a wolf, if he showed good taste, would let me alone, and wait for you, Bumpus," Giraffe called back.

They hastened to deposit their burdens under the shelving rock.

"Now, Thad, don't you think it'd be a good idea to have everybody hustle, and collect what fuel we could?" the fire-maker asked.

"As it's apt to rain any, time now," answered the scout-master, "and we'll be glad to have a fire all night, it seems as though we'd show our good sense by gathering wood while we have the chance."

"That's the ticket! You hear Thad speaking, fellows, so get busy."

Giraffe showed them how by immediately starting in to collect such wood as lay conveniently at hand.

"Pile it up here, where it'll keep dry, and we can get what we need from time to time," he told them.

Many hands make light work, and as the entire half dozen boys busied themselves like a pack of beavers, before long they had accumulated such a pile of good dry fuel as pleased Giraffe exceedingly.

"That's what I call a hunky-dory lot of wood," he finally declared, when Thad had announced the they must surely have enough to see them through the night, "but better bring in a little more, boys, because you don't know how fast the fire eats it up."

As for himself, Giraffe was now ready to get his cheery blaze started.

He actually wasted a match in doing this, muttering at the time that there was no use bothering with his fire-sticks, which would come in handy later, perhaps, when the stock of matches ran low.

Well, every boy admitted that things certainly did take on a rosier hue, once that fire began to crackle and send up sparks.

"That feels good, Giraffe," said Bumpus, holding his hands out toward the blaze.

"Sure it does," the fire maker went on to say, "and we'll all feel better still after we get some grub inside. Thad, what are we going to have for supper?"

Nobody started making fun of Giraffe now. They were all pretty sharp pushed, and could sympathize with the hungry one.

"Oh! look over our stock, and see what we've got," replied the scout-master. "Only go slow, and don't cook too much, because nobody can tell how long we might have to stay here on this island, and we may have to come down to half rations yet."

His words struck a chill to some of their hearts.

Giraffe, however, refused to allow himself to be concerned.

"Oh! don't worry, boys," he remarked, "we ain't going to starve, even if we have to be marooned here two weeks before a vessel can be signaled. Why, what use are the fishing lines to us if we can't take lots of finny prizes? Then, if there's ducks around, or anything else to shoot, ain't we got a gun? And last of all, I reckon we'd find lots of mussels or fresh water clams in the sand at the end of the island where we landed."

Somehow, his hopeful spirit did a great deal to help buoy up the spirits of the other scouts.

Even Bumpus volunteered to assist in getting supper ready; indeed, there was no lack of cooks on this occasion, for every one seemed willing to lend a hand.

After all, youth is so hopeful, and filled with animal spirits, that it takes more than ordinary backsets to dishearten a parcel of healthy boys.

By the time the supper was done they were talking like magpies, and it would be difficult to imagine that these six happy-go-lucky fellows were now actual Crusoes of the great lake, their boat a wreck, and deliverance a very uncertain prospect of the future.

"That's the very last of the bacon, ain't it, Giraffe?" asked Step Hen, during the progress of the meal.

"Sorry to say it is," came the reply.

"And don't it taste finer than ever, though?" Bumpus wanted to know.

"That's always the way," laughed Thad.

"Yes," added Allan, "you never miss the water till the well runs dry.

But how about our ham, is that gone, too!"

"Well, I should say, yes," declared Giraffe, an injured look on his face, as if he felt accusing eyes fixed upon him, "s'pose you think one poor lone ham with six hungry fellows to chaw away at it, could last forever, but it won't. If you want to know what we've got left I'll tell you—two cans of Boston baked beans, one of tomatoes, some potatoes, a package of rice, plenty of tea, sugar and coffee, three tins of milk, some chocolate, and three packages of crackers."

"Is that all?" gasped Bumpus.

"So you see right away to-morrow we've got to get busy trying to lay in some sort of supplies," Giraffe went on to say. "How about that, Thad?"

"You never said truer words," was the scoutmaster's comment.

"Yum, yum, I don't know when I've enjoyed a supper like I have this one," Step Hen acknowledged.

"I hope it ain't the last time I'll hear you say that," remarked

Giraffe.

"Hope so myself," returned the other, "because it'd be too bad if I had to quit eating at my tender age."

"Thad, do you think this island could be inhabited?"

It was Davy who asked this question, but Bumpus must have been thinking along the same lines, for he nodded his head violently and smiled, as though he awaited Thad's answer with interest.

"Of course I couldn't say," the scout-master observed. "It's only a small rocky island, you know, and people wouldn't live here the year' through."

"But they might come here, ain't that so?" Step Hen insisted.

"Why, yes, to fish, or shoot wild fowl in the season," Thad went on to say.

"Well, I sure do hope there may be some white fish netters here right now," Step Hen said.

"Or if their ain't, let's wish they'll be comin' along soon," Bumpus added with a fervency that was certainly genuine.

"I wonder," Davy broke in with, "what we could do if our boat was carried away, or we found we couldn't mend the same?"

"Huh! What did old Robinson do but build him a boat? Here are six boys, wide-awake as they make 'em—and I'd like to know why we couldn't do as much as one man!"

Bumpus said this rather boastfully, not that he had so much confidence in his own ability to do things as he felt satisfied that Thad and Allan would be equal to almost any emergency.

"Well, we might, under the same conditions," the former told him.

"Ain't the conditions the same," inquired Step Hen. "He was wrecked, and so are we, you might call it."

"Yes, but there's no tree on this rocky island big enough to make into a boat," Thad informed him.

"That's a fact, they do grow dwarf trees here," Step Hen admitted.

"And suppose there was, how could we ever chop one down with one little camp hatchet, and hollow out the log?" Thad asked.

"Might take a year," acknowledged the other.

"We'd freeze to death here in the winter time, because it gets awful cold, they say," Step Hen continued.

"Why, we could walk over the ice, and get ashore," Davy suggested.

"Guess the old lake don't freeze over solid any time; it's too big, ain't it, Thad?" Giraffe went on to say.

"That's something I don't know," came the scout master's answer; "and what's more to the point I don't care, because we'll never stay here that long."

"Glad to know it," said Bumpus. "P'raps now our friends'll be looking us up, and come to the rescue."

"You mean Smithy and Bob White, don't you?" asked Step Hen.

"That's who."

And so they continued to discuss matters from every view-point possible, as only wide-awake boys may.

Meanwhile the scout-master, thinking that while the rain held off he might as well step out and take a little look around, proceeded to do so.

Allan Hollister was sitting there, resting, and listening to the arguments of the other boys, when he saw the scout-master beckoning just outside the full glow of light cast by the fire.

"What's up, Thad?" he asked, as he joined the other.

"I think I've made the discovery that we're not alone on the island," came the answer.

CHAPTER XVIII

WHAT THAD FOUND OUT

"That sounds good to me, Thad," remarked Allan.

"Hold on before you say that," the other went on to say, significantly.

"What about it?" demanded Allan.

"Because we don't know who they may be, if there are men out here," answered the cautious scout-master.

The other gave a low whistle that stood for surprise.

"I see now, what you mean," he observed; "but what makes you think there are others here, when they never lifted a hand to help us, and haven't as much as dropped in to sit at our fire?"

"Well, perhaps they don't want to see us," Thad told him.

"Oh! yes, we were talking about smugglers, and then we ran across that Mr. Stebbins who knew all about us, and he was one of a party looking up the slick men who fetch things over from Canada to escape the heavy duties. But Thad do you, really believe there could be a bunch of that stripe hiding out on Sturgeon Island?"

"I don't know anything yet, Allan, except that I've reason to know we're not alone out here, that's all."

"Well, what did you see, or hear?" asked the other.

"This is what happened," Thad went on to say, in a low tone, though the storm was still making such a racket that he had to put his mouth close to Allan's ear in order to allow him to catch what he said. "While the rest kept up their talking I came out here to see how things looked, and make up my mind whether we were going to have any wet with this gale or not."

"Yes, and it don't look like it now, Thad, because it's gone so far; reckon it must be what they call a dry storm; but go on and tell me the rest."

"Well, I was standing about here, in the dense shadow, you see, thinking, when all at once I discovered that there was something moving between me and the fire!"

"Whew!" murmured Allan, deeply impressed.

"Of course, at first I thought it might be only a fox, or something like that, curious enough to want to creep up, and learn what sort of intruders had landed on Sturgeon Island; I could see that the bushes were moving softly, and that soon the thing, whatever it was, would come in sight of where stood here."

"And it did?" Allan demanded.

"That's right," replied the other, softly; "and it turned out to be a man's head!"

At that the other scout again gave one of his low whistles, to show that he was listening, and duly impressed by the startling information conveyed.

"Of course," continued Thad, "I couldn't make out what he was like, very well, because his face was turned away from me; but as near as I can say he was a big man, a rough looking chap, and ugly in the bargain. More than that, he struck me like he might be a half-breed, or else an Italian, for his skin was very dark."

"Well, what did he do?" inquired the other.

"Just lay there watching the rest of you for several minutes, Allan. I could see him elevate his head at times, and then duck like a flash when he thought some one might be looking his way; which showed pretty plainly that he didn't want to be seen, and that he didn't mean to step forward and join the crowd."

"Then he went away, did he?" continued the other.

"Yes, backed off, and I lost track of him among the rocks and the bushes," Thad went on to say, impressively. "It struck me as a queer proceeding, and I didn't lose much time in getting you out here, so I could talk it over."

"Perhaps there's only one, all told, and he might be some fellow who's escaped from prison, and is in hiding away off here, where he thinks no one will ever take the trouble to look for him," Allan suggested.

The scout-master shook his head.

"I can't say just what he is, or whether there's a dozen here," he observed; "but I do know that all his actions were suspicious, for no honest fisherman would do what he did."

"We'll have to be on our guard, then, Thad?"

"That goes without saying, until we know more about who our neighbors are," the scout-master replied.

"It sort of complicates the situation some, too, don't it?" Allan asked.

"Yes, and perhaps we'd better not say anything to the rest until we learn something more about this thing," Thad told him.

"How are you going to do that, when this man seems disposed to give us the cold-shoulder?" inquired the other.

"I had about made up my mind to go off for a little stroll, and see what I could run across near by," the scout-master continued. "This island isn't so very large but I could find my way around; and while that storm is howling I'm not anxious to cross over to the other side. This is the sheltered part, and like as not these people, whoever they turn out to be, will have taken up their camp somewhere about here. But I wanted to warn you so you might make sure none of the other fellows wandered off."

"I'll see to it, though I don't think they're apt to do anything of that sort, as they're a tired bunch right now," Allan assured him.

"And while you're about it," continued the other, impressively, "you'd better keep your hand on that shotgun of ours all the while, until you see me beckon to you again."

"That sounds like you expected we'd be up against it good and hard before this game came to an end," remarked Allan.

"Oh! not necessarily," replied his chum. "It's only following out our motto, 'be prepared.' You know there are a whole lot of sayings along that line, such as 'fore-warned is fore-armed,' and as the old pilgrim fathers used to say: 'trust in the Lord; but, keep your powder dry!' We want to keep our ammunition ready. But while you go back to the rest of the boys I'll take a sneak."

"Don't think you'd better take that gun along with you, Thad?"

"Not at all," was the quick reply. "I'll depend on the darkness, and the noise of the storm, to keep from being seen or heard. But I'm bent on trying to find out whether there's any sort of shack or cabin built here on Sturgeon Island.

"Well, take good care of yourself," warned Allan, a little uneasily; for it was almost on his lips to ask why he might not be permitted to keep the scout-master company, for he did hate so much to see Thad pull out alone.

He insisted on gravely shaking hands before he would leave his partner, to return to the camp under the rocky shelf. They had been so much together of recent years that these two boys were exceedingly fond of each other, more so than brothers could ever have been; which was one reason why Allan disliked seeing the other moving away into the darkness, and taking voluntarily upon himself the dangers such a scout involved.

Obeying orders he himself made his way back to where the other sat. Giraffe was holding out, and explaining something that he had advanced; but evidently he must have noticed the absence of the others, for he soon asked:

"What's the good word, Allan; because I reckon you and our scout-master have been taking a squint at the weather? I was just telling the rest here that we won't get any wet with this blow, because all the signs point that way, and as I said before. I'm getting to be an authority on weather now-a-days.

"That was about what we thought," Allan told him.

"You mean that Thad is with me in my assertion, do you?" demanded Giraffe; and when the other had nodded in the affirmative the tall scout turned to Davy, Bumpus and Step Hen triumphantly, to add: "There, didn't I tell you I could hit these weather changes on the handle every time. When I warn you next time there's going to be a storm, better hurry to get in out of the wet."

"I think it's a great pity you waste your precious time bothering about what the weather is agoing to be, when we can't help it; and you might be racking that really stupendous brain of yours adoing other things worth while," Bumpus went on to remark.

"Huh! as what?" Giraffe wanted to know.

"Well, famines in the eating line, for one thing," spoke up the fat scout, instantly. "S'pose now you'd told us we was going to run up against hard times, in the way of a scarcity of grub two days back, couldn't we just as well have dropped in to some town along the shore, and stacked up with heaps and heaps of good things? Seems to me, Giraffe, you've gone and wasted your talent on the wrong thing. What good is it ever agoing to do you, to pretend to tell what sort of weather we'll get next week, when it's only a guess after all? Better make a change, and predict famines and such things, so we can take the alarm, and buy out some country grocery."

Giraffe had not one word to say in reply. He must have recognized the force of Bumpus' philosophy, and wished in his heart he had been gifted with the spirit of prophecy, so that he might have given warning in due time as to the need of replenishing their stock of provisions.

The conversation ran on, other subjects being taken up. Giraffe wanted to know what kept Thad away so long, and was told that the scout-master had concluded to take a little look around.

At that the other suggested that perhaps he too might stretch his legs; whereupon Allan informed him that he was under orders to keep them all close to the ledge under which they had found shelter; and that Thad had told him no one must be allowed to stray away a single yard.

After that the boys did not talk quite so volubly; possibly some suspicion may have entered their minds that perhaps things were not quite so peaceful as they appeared on the surface; and that Thad might know of some reason for expecting a new batch of troubles to descend upon them.

Allan kept sitting there, gun in hand. He was waiting to receive some sort of sign from Thad, to tell him his presence was desired once again out there beside the tree where they had previously conferred.

It seemed a very long time before he caught a movement there, and then saw the hand of the scout-master beckoning to him.

"Stay here, as Thad wants to talk with me," he told the rest, after which he strode forth to join the other.

"Well, did you find out anything?" he asked, the first thing.

"Only this," replied Thad, solemnly, "the island is occupied by a party of several rough men, who have a boat in a sheltered cove over there, and a cabin half hidden among the rocks and brushwood; but the mystery of it all is, what they may be doing here, and why they look on us as enemies!"

CHAPTER XIX

BAD NEIGHBORS

"It seems to be getting worse and worse, the further we go, don't it, Thad?" Allan asked, after he had had time to digest the startling information which his chum had imparted, as they stood there within the outer edge of the glow cast by Giraffe's camp-fire under the overhanging ledge of rock.

"Looks that way," replied the other, seriously enough, for he did not exactly like the situation.

"Seems like it wasn't bad enough for us to be wrecked, and marooned on this queer island, but we have to fall across the trail of some unknown parties who may be up to all sorts of unlawful dodges, for all we know. But Thad, tell me more of what you saw and heard."

"When I started out from here," the scoutmaster began, "I knew that I'd probably only have to look around at this end of the island, because no sensible man was going to take up his quarters where these storms always strike in. And then I figured it out that the chances were, these parties, if there were more than the one fellow I'd seen sneaking around, and spying on us, would want to be down close to the water, for a good many reasons. You can understand that, Allan?"

"Yes, and I think that notion would have come to me, just as it did you," replied the other promptly, showing that he was following the narrative closely.

"Well, that being the case," resumed the scoutmaster, "I stuck to the lower part of the land, climbing over and around such outcropping rocks as I came across. The moon wasn't helping me very much, though it's up there behind the clouds; and on that account you see the darkness is never so bad as when there's no moon at all.

"It wasn't so very long before I heard something knocking softly near by, and listening carefully I made up my mind that it must be a boat that was kept in a snug cove perhaps, and yet where it got more or less wash of the sea beyond.

"That was just what it turned out to be, Allan, a fair sized motorboat, stoutly built, and yet something of a hummer when it would come to speed. Her outlines told me this as soon as I could make her out down in the berth she occupied between the rocks where they had protected the sides of the little basin with logs to keep her from chafing too much.

"Now, speed indicates that the people owning that boat expect to show a clean pair of heels, as they say, at times. They want to be in condition to skip out in a hurry, and be able to outrun any ordinary craft that might try to overhaul them. Wouldn't you think that way, Allan?"

"You're speaking my mind to a dot, Thad."

"But I wasn't satisfied wholly, and made another move, to see whether they had any sort of a cabin around. Seemed to me that if they were using Sturgeon Island for some sort of shady business, they ought to have a shelter. Well, I found it before ten minutes had passed, and by just creeping along what I made out to be a regular trail leading from the boat up the shore a piece."

"Good for you, Thad; no woodsman could have done better!" exclaimed the other scout, who, having had practical experience extending through many trips into the wilderness with hunting parties, was pretty well posted on the numerous little "wrinkles" connected with woods lore.

"Oh! that was the most natural thing in the world for any one to do, and I don't deserve any credit, Allan. But there were times when I admit I did have to almost smell that trail, for it passed over little stretches of rock, you see. At such times I had to look around, guess about where it ought to be found where the earth began again, and in that way pick it up once more."

"And it really led you to a cabin, did it?" Allan asked, as the other paused.

"Yes, and there had been a fire burning in front of the shack, though I found only the ashes, as though it had been-hurriedly put out, perhaps when they first saw us heading toward the island, just before the storm came along."

"The ashes were still warm, then?" queried Allan, knowing that to be the logical way a forest ranger always learns about how long past a fire has burned out, or been extinguished.

"They were, and I could see that the brands had been torn apart, showing that some one was in a hurry to keep its light from betraying the fact of any person being camped on Sturgeon Island."

"Just what I'd think myself, Thad."

"After I saw that there was a cabin," continued the scout-master, "I wondered whether I had better take chances, and crawl up close enough to hear what they were saying, if so be there were men there. Before I had gone far in that scheme I realized that it was a little too risky, because I could hear a moving about, as though several men might be passing in and out. I also caught an occasional low muttering tone; but the noise of the waves dashing against the rocks, and the rattling of the branches of the trees that overhung the lone cabin, kept me from catching more than a single word now and then.

"After listening for quite a while I thought you would be getting anxious about my staying so long; and as I couldn't get any real satisfaction out of the game by hanging around any longer, why, I made up my mind to clear out. I'd learned several things, anyway, and by putting our heads together thought we might get at the meat in the cocoanut."

Of course that was a neat way of admitting that he wanted to talk matters over with his best chum, on the supposition that "two heads are better than one." Allan took it that way, for had he not on numberless occasions done just about the same thing?

"Of course you couldn't tell how many of these men there were, Thad?" he asked.

"I tried to make a stab at it by noticing the different sound of voices; and I'm dead sure there must have been three anyhow, p'raps more," the scout-master told him.

"And I think you've said once or twice that they seemed to be a rough lot?" the other went on to remark.

"That's my impression, Allan, from a number of things which I won't bother mentioning now. And there's something more. I told you that when I had a glimpse of the fellow who spied on our camp I thought he might be a foreigner, or a half-breed, didn't I?"

"Yes, I remember you did, Thad."

"Well," explained the other, "although I heard so poorly while I was hanging out near that hidden shack there were times when I thought one of the men was talking in some tongue besides plain United States. Fact is, he rattled off something in French."

"Oh! then it's plain who they are—half-breed Canadians from the North Shore. As this island properly belongs to Canada they would have a right to land here, and our coming needn't bother them any—if they are honest men."

"Thad, they wouldn't hide out like they do if they were the right sort. Make up your mind they're doing something that's against the law. Honest men don't carry on this way, and spy on a camp of Boy Scouts wrecked in a storm. Why, no matter how rough they might be, they'd drop in on us, and offer to share whatever they had. It's only fear of arrest that makes cowards of men this way."

"I forgot to tell you that among the few words I did manage to pick up by straining my ears to the limit, were just three that gave me an idea they took us for a detachment of militia, either Canadian or Yankee, out on the lake on some serious business that might interfere with their trade. Those three words were 'soldiers,' 'khaki,' and 'arrest.'"

Allan gave a soft whistle to indicate how his state of feeling corresponded with that of his chum.

"There isn't any doubt about it in my mind, Thad," he asserted, vehemently; "but that they're here for no good. That fast launch means they are in the habit of making swift trips back and forth, perhaps taking the night for it every time, so as to run less chance of being seen. And here hard luck has marooned us on Sturgeon Island with a bunch of desperate smugglers, who look on us as soldiers sent out by the Government to gather them in. If ever we were up against it hard, we sure are right now, Pard Thad."

"You seem to have set your mind on that one explanation of their presence here; and I'll admit that this island would be a great half-way place to hide the smuggled goods on, till the right night came to run them across to the American shore; but perhaps you're barking up the wrong tree there, Allan!"

"Oh! I'll admit that when I call them smugglers I'm only guessing, because, so far as I know we haven't any sort of evidence looking that way. It only seems the most natural explanation of why they're so much afraid of us, believing as they seem to that we're connected with the Government, one side or the other, just on account of these Boy Scout uniforms, which I reckon they don't happen to be familiar with. But Thad, you're holding something back; I can tell that by the way you act. You learned more than you've told me so far; own up to that."

The young scout-master chuckled. He liked to spring little surprises once in a while. It was just like tapping a peg until he had it set in the ground to suit his fancy; and then with one master-stroke driving it home. He had whetted Allan's curiosity now, and the time had come to satisfy it.

"Yes," Thad went on to say, "there was one little discovery I made that gave me certain information, and it was strong enough to convince me that our earlier suspicions about smugglers and all that sort of thing were away off the track."

"Yes, go on, please, Thad."

"It struck me while I was lying there not so very far away from that shanty hidden among the rocks and brushwood. Most of the time the wind was blowing on my left side, but every little while there would come a pucker or a flaw, causing it to change for just for a second or two. And it was when this happened the first time I got scent of what was in the wind, in a double sense. In other words, Allan, I discovered a distinct odor of fish in the air!"

"Oh! now I tumble to what you mean!" exclaimed the other.

"And every time that wind brought me a whiff of the fishy smell the stronger became my conviction that these men must be poachers, who knew they were breaking certain game laws by taking white fish or trout illegally, and reaping a harvest that honest fishermen were unable to reach. Stop and think if things don't point that way?"

And Allan did not have to hesitate in the least, for what his companion had just told him seemed to settle the matter beyond all dispute.

"Yes, Thad," he said, "now you've let the cat out of the bag there can't be any question about it. These half-breed Canadians are illegal fishermen, poachers they'd be called up in Maine; and they believe we've come to arrest the lot. It's a bad lookout for the Silver Fox Patrol; but we've seen worse, and always came out on top."

CHAPTER XX

"HOLD THE FORT!"

As a rule it did not take these boys long to decide upon their course of action. And in the present instance they had so little choice that unusually prompt results might be expected.

"We'd better tell the other fellows, to begin with?" ventured Allan.

"Yes," remarked the scout-master, promptly, "it wouldn't be fair to keep things like this from the boys. They're just as much interested in how it turns out as we are. And, besides, we may get a bright idea from somebody."

"You never can tell," added Allan; and some of those same other scouts might not have felt complimented could they have heard him say these words, as they seemed to imply that miracles did sometimes happen, when you were least expecting them.

But having made up their minds on this score the pair walked over to the camp under that friendly ledge.

Upon their arrival every eye was immediately glued upon Thad. It seemed as though Giraffe, Bumpus, Davy and Step Hen must have guessed that the scout-master had made some sort of exciting discovery, and now meant to take them into his confidence.

Complete silence greeted the arrival of the two who had been conferring so mysteriously near by. Of course, once Thad broke the ice, and started to tell what he had discovered, this was apt to give way to a bombardment of questions; for Giraffe and Bumpus could think up the greatest lot of "wants" imaginable; so that it would keep Thad busy explaining, until their ammunition ran out, or he had to throw up his hands in surrender through sheer exhaustion.

He started in to explain what he had seen, and done, as soon as he dropped down beside his comrades of the Silver Fox Patrol. Immediately he had the attention of every one enlisted. Bumpus sat there, watching and listening with such intentness that you would hardly believe he breathed at all. Step Hen, too, was following every word spoken by the scout-master, as though trying to grasp the seriousness of the situation, and figure out a way to circumvent the danger that had arisen so unexpectedly in their path. And the other two could not be said to be far behind in the interest they betrayed.

As we have already heard Thad tell Allan about his first, seeing the man who was spying upon the camp; and later on how he came to find the hidden boat, as well as the concealed cabin, there is no necessity for us to follow the scout-master while he imparts this information to the quartette who, having been absent from that interview, had no previous knowledge of the facts.

By the time he spoke of crawling silently away, and coming back to join the balance of the patrol, he had his chums worked up to a feverish pitch of excitement.

"Well," Step Hen was the first to break in with, "anyhow, game-fish poachers ain't quite so bad as smugglers would have been, and that's one satisfaction, I take it."

"But they're bad enough," urged Davy; "because they must be breaking the laws by taking fish in some way that ain't allowed. And if trapped they stand a chance to face a heavy fine, or a long sentence in jail, perhaps both. And if, as Thad says, they've got the silly idea in their heads that we're connected with the Canadian militia, and came here meaning to destroy their nets, and likewise haul the men over the coals, why, they'll either skedaddle and leave us marooned on old Sturgeon for keeps, or else do something worse."

"What sort of worse, Davy?" demanded Bumpus. "There you go again, saying things in a sort of half-cooked way, and leaving the rest to a fellow's wild imagination. Do you mean you believe they'd really hurt us, when we ain't so much as lifted a finger to do the bunch any harm? Speak out and tell us, now, you old croaker."

"Thad, what do you think they might do?" Davy asked, under the impression that he would be wise to leave the explanation of the matter to one who was more capable of handling it than he could possibly be.

"If they were sensible men," remarked the other, deliberately, as though he had given that particular thought much attention, "I wouldn't be afraid, because then we could reason with them, and explain that we were only a party of the Boy Scouts of America, off on a little cruise, and shipwrecked in the storm; also, that if they helped us in any way we'd just forget that we'd ever seen them here."

"But explain and tell us what you mean by hinting that they mightn't be sensible men?" remarked Step Hen.

"Oh! well, that was my way of putting it," Thad went on to say; "I meant that as near as I could guess they seem to be Canadian half-breeds, for some of their talk was in a French patois I couldn't just understand. And I've always heard that those kind of men are mighty hard to handle, because, like Italians they get furiously excited, and let their imaginations run away with them, like some other fellows I happen to know."

"Did you say there, were only three of this bad crowd, Thad?" Giraffe asked.

"I wouldn't like to say for sure," came the reply, "but as near as I could make out that would cover the bill."

"Huh! and we count six, all told," continued the tall scout, indifferently, although Thad imagined he was not feeling so comfortable as he pretended to be.

"Yes, six boys," the scout-master reminded him.

"But husky boys in the bargain, and accustomed to taking care of themselves in tight places," Giraffe went on to remark, proudly. "Besides, ain't we got a gun that shoots twice? That ought to account for a couple of the rascals; and then what would one poor fish poacher be against a half dozen lively fellows, tell me that?"

Allan laughed at hearing the boast.

"How easy it is to figure out who's going to win the next championship in the National League of baseball clubs, while you're sitting around the stove in the winter time?" he told Giraffe. "But these paper victories seldom pan out the same way when the good old summer time comes along, and the boys get hustling. I suppose now, Giraffe, you'll be the one to knock over those two men, each with a single shot from your faithful double-barrel. Give him the gun, Step Hen, and let him start in right away."

Of course that rather startled the tall scout.

"Hold on there, don't be in such a big hurry!" he went on to say, holding up a hand to persuade Step Hen to keep the firearm a while longer. "Course now I didn't exactly mean it that way. I never wanted to shoot a man, that I know of. What I had in my mind, I reckon, was that one of us could keep a pair of these rascals covered with the shotgun, and hold 'em steady, while the other five managed the third of the bunch. See?"

"The trouble is," Thad told them, "none of us know French, and in that case we mightn't be able to talk with the poachers, even if they gave us half a chance. They seem to have a bad case of the rattles right now, and if it wasn't for the storm I really believe they'd get away from here in a hurry."

"Do we want 'em to go, or stay?" asked Bumpus, as though he could not settle in his own mind which one of these several openings would be best for their interests.

"For my part," spoke up Step Hen, "they couldn't clear out any too soon to make me feel happy. I know what the breed is like, and believe me, boys, I don't care to make their acquaintance, not me."

"That's all mighty fine, Step Hen," remarked Giraffe, loftily, "but when you talk that way you don't look far enough ahead."

"Just explain that, will you, and tell me why I don't?" demanded the other, with some show of indignation.

"Well, suppose now they did jump the island, and give us the merry ha! ha! what difference would it make to us whether they upset out there on that stormy lake or not; wouldn't we lose all chance of being ferried across to the mainland, and so making our escape from this measly island?"

Step Hen apparently caught the force of this reasoning, for he subsided, with a sort of discontented grunt.

Davy, however, took up the reasoning at this point.

"But suppose now they wouldn't want to get out in such a hurry? What if they had a lot of valuable fish nets around somewhere that they hated to let go? Don't you reckon in that case they might take a notion to try and bag the lot of us, so's to hold us prisoners till they could decide what to do with the ones they took to be Government spies?"

Bumpus groaned as he listened to all this terrible talk. His mind was already on fire with anticipations of what the immediate future might bring forth. Still, on occasion Bumpus could show considerable valor; and several times in the past he had astonished his chums by certain feats which he had engineered.

"It's up to me to think up some way to get us out of this terrible pickle," he was telling himself, over and over again; but even if any one of his five comrades heard what he was saying they paid little attention to it; but the fat scout meant all he said, as the future proved.

"One thing sure," Giraffe went on to remark, presently, "they know where our little camp is, because Thad saw that spy watching what we was adoing here. And if so be they should take a notion to pay us a visit before morning, why, they wouldn't have any trouble finding us out."

"Not less we made a move," argued Davy.

"And we're too nicely fixed here for that, ain't we?" Giraffe demanded, as he cast a swift look around to where the various blankets, having first been dried in the heat of the fire, were now inviting to repose, each fellow having apparently selected the particular spot where he meant to sleep, let the wind howl as hard as it wished, for that projecting rocky ledge would keep any rain from coming in upon them.

"That's right, Giraffe; you know a good thing when you see it!" declared Bumpus, who did not altogether fancy starting out to seek another camp, where they would have to lie down in the dark, and take chances of being caught in a rain, if later on such a change in the character of the storm came about.

"Then, if Thad says the word, we'll stick right here, and hold the fort!" the tall scout exclaimed. "In the words of that immortal Scot we read about, what was his name, Roderick Dhu, I think, who cried: 'Sooner will this rock fly from its firm base, than I.' Them's our sentiments, ain't they, fellows?"

"Hear! Hear!" came from Bumpus, as he snuggled down again contentedly, believing that this disagreeable part of the program at least had been indefinitely postponed, and that they stood a good chance for staying out their time under that friendly protecting ledge.

CHAPTER XXI

GIRAFFE HAS A SCHEME

"If they'd only leave us alone, why, what's to hinder us mending our own ship, and sailing away out of this, sooner or later?" Bumpus wanted to know; after they had been talking the matter over for a long time.

"I suppose you'll do the mending part, Bumpus?" demanded Step Hen, wickedly.

"Well, I'd be only too willing, if I knew how," instantly flashed back the other, "but unfortunately my education was neglected when it came to patching up boats, and tinkering with machinery. I'm ashamed to confess to that, but it's the whole sad truth. But, thank goodness, we've got a scoutmaster who can do the job mighty near as well as any machinist going. I'll back Thad, yes, and Allan in the bargain, to make a decent job of it. And even Giraffe here might fix things up in a pinch. So long as we've got a chance to make the Chippeway Belle do duty again at the old stand we hadn't ought to complain, I think, boys."

"I'm sorry to tell you that there's only a slim chance of that ever coming about," Thad remarked, right then and there.

"Then you believe she was smashed worse'n any of us thought was the case; is that it, Thad?" asked Giraffe.

"No, it isn't that so much as another thing I've noticed lately, that's going to upset our calculations," replied the scout-master.

"Tell us what that might be, won't you?" pleaded Bumpus, with a doleful shake of his head; as though he might be beginning to believe in the truth of that old saying to the effect that "troubles never come singly."

"You may remember," Thad went on to say, "that when you asked my opinion be fore about the boat staying where we left it, I said there was a good chance we'd find her there in the morning if the wind didn't shift?"

"And now you mean that it's doing that very same thing, do you?" Giraffe asked.

"If you'd taken the trouble to notice all sorts of things, that you had always ought to as a true scout," the other told him, "you'd have found that out for yourself. The fact of the matter is that when we first reached this place under the ledge the wind seemed to find a way in here, and make the fire flare at times. Look at it now, and you'll see that it's as steady as anything; yet you can hear the rush of the wind through the treetops just the same. It's turned around as much as twenty degrees, I should say."

105

"And that's bad for the boat, ain't it?" Bumpus wanted to know.

"I'm afraid so," the scout-master replied; "because it will get the full force of both wind and heavy seas. Long before morning it will most likely be carried out into deep water, and disappear from sight. I think we've seen the last of the Chippeway Belle, boys."

"But, Thad," observed Giraffe, "how about that anchor rope? You know we carried it ashore, and fastened it to a rock. Would that break, now? It was a dandy rope, and nearly new."

"Well," said Thad, decisively, "once the seas begin to pound against the boat, with every wave the strain on that rope is bound to be just terrific. It might hold for a time; but mark my words, the constant chafing against the rock, where you fastened the end, will wear the strands until they snap; and then good-bye to our boat."

"Then we had better make up our minds to facing that fact, and not feel very much disappointed if in the morning we can't see a sign of the Belle," Allan went on to give, as his opinion; for he accepted, the theory advanced by the scout-master as though there could be no reasonable doubt about its being a positive fad.

"What if them fellows took a notion to step in on us to-night, and make us all prisoners of war?" queried Bumpus; for this possibility had been working overtime in his brain, and he was only waiting for a break in the conversation to advance it.

"Just what I was going to speak about," Giraffe up and said, somewhat excitedly. "You all sat down on me when I happened to remark about getting a pair of the birds with the gun. I move that we ask Thad to take charge of the firearm, and the rest can load up with whatsoever they can find," and leaning over, he deliberately appropriated the camp hatchet before Step Hen, whose eye had immediately started to look for the same, could fasten, upon it.

"Me too, I second the motion!" exclaimed Davy, in turn making a dive for the long and dangerous looking bread knife, which had proved so handy for many services while on the trip, and was being constantly lost and found again.

"But where do I come in?" asked Bumpus, as he saw the favorite weapons of offense and defense taken possession of so rapidly.

"A club will do for you, and Step Hen as well," remarked Giraffe, complacently; "for when a fellow has appropriated the best there is, he can afford to smile at his less fortunate comrades, and assume a superior air.

"Oh! well, I'd just as soon arm myself that way," the fat scout told them, as he set about finding something that would answer the purpose from amidst the firewood they had carried under the ledge to keep it from getting wet. "I'm a peaceful fellow, as you all know, and think there's nothing like a good hickory or oak club to convince other people that you've got rights you want them to respect. I've practiced swinging Indian clubs by the hour; and when it comes to giving a right hard smack, count me in. That's going to hurt, without injury to body or limb."

At another and less exciting time Giraffe would have surely insisted upon Bumpus explaining the difference, between these two sources of injury; but just then he had too much else to bother his head about to start an argument.

"Now, let's see any three men tackle this crowd, that's what!" he went on to remark, as he swept his eye proudly over the motley array of weapons; for even Allan had armed himself, having a stout stick, with which he doubtless felt able to render a good account of himself in a tussle.

"But let's remember," warned Thad, "that we don't want to let ourselves be drawn into a battle with these poachers, unless it's the last resort. They're ignorant men, and just now they must feel pretty desperate, thinking that we're going to break up a profitable game they've been playing for a long time, carrying their fish to some American market against the laws of Canada, and perhaps smuggling their cargo in, if there's any duty on fish, which I don't know about."

"If only you could get a bare chance to talk with one of the lot, Thad," Allan spoke up, "I'm pretty sure you'd be able to let them know the truth; and in that way we'd perhaps make friends of them. They might take our solemn promise that we never would give them away, and land us somewhere ashore, so we could make our way to either Duluth, or some other place to the north here."

"I'm hoping to get just such an opening, if we can hold the fort till morning; and they haven't skipped out by then," Thad told him; which proved that he had planned far ahead of anything that had as yet been proposed.

"And meanwhile try to be thinking up any French words you ever heard," suggested Bumpus, artfully. "Who knows what use the same'd be to you in a tight hole. How'd parley vous Francais sound, now? I've heard our dancing-master in Cranford use that more'n a few times, though I own up I don't know from Adam what she means. But it might make a fellow come to a standstill if he was agoing to run you through, and you suddenly shot it at him."

"Thank you, Bumpus, I'll remember that, though I think it means 'do you speak French?' And what if he took me up, and became excited because I couldn't understand anything he said, you see it wouldn't help much," the scout-master told him.

"But say, what are we meaning to do about standing guard; because I reckon now we've got to watch out, and not let them fellows gobble us up while we're sleeping like the babes in the wood?" Step Hen asked.

"Oh! that can be fixed easy enough, if we all have to stay awake through the whole night. Wouldn't that be the best plan, Thad?"

It was Bumpus who put this important question, but none of them were deceived in the least by this apparent warlike aspect on the part of the fat scout.

Bumpus could play a clever game when he became fully aroused; but if Thad guessed what his true reason might be for asking such a question, he did not choose to betray the fact, knowing that it would cause the fat scout more or less confusion.

"Yes, it might be as well for all of us to try and stay awake!" he declared. "As you seem to have settled it that the gun falls to my share, why, I'll make up my mind not to close an eye the whole livelong night; and if the rest choose to sit up with me and help watch, the more the merrier."

"I will, for one," said Giraffe, stoutly.

"You can count on me to make the try," added Davy.

"Ditto here," Allan went on to say.

"Oh! I'm willing enough," Bumpus observed hastily, seeing that several of his comrades were waiting for him to speak; "but I hope that every time anybody just sees me abobbing my head he'll stick a pin in me; only please don't jab it too deep, or you'll make me howl."

"As for me," Step Hen added, "I don't feel a whit sleepy right now; and my eyes are as starey as a cat's, or Jim's over yonder," pointing to where he had managed to fasten the captive owl, which he had persisted in carrying ashore, despite the fact that he had about all the burden any boy would care to carry when compelled to wade through water almost up to his neck.

"Well, listen here, then," remarked Giraffe, mysteriously, "I've been thinking up a scheme that looks good to me, and I want to know how the rest of you stand when it comes to trying it out."

"Go on and tell us what it is, Giraffe!" exclaimed Bumpus, eagerly.

"Yes, if you have thought up anything worth while, we'd be mighty glad to hear about the same," added Allan.

The tall scout looked cautiously about him, and lowering his voice went on:

"Why, I'll tell you, fellows, what I thought. Now, about that boat belonging to these here poachers, what's to hinder us from coolly appropriating the same, and starting out to look for the mainland ourselves? Then, you see, it'll be that bunch that's left behind to be marooners on old Sturgeon Island; and when we get to town why, we can let the authorities know all about what they're adoing out here, so they'll come and arrest the whole kit. Now, what d'ye say about that for an idea, hey?"

CHAPTER XXII

THE LONG NIGHT

"Good for you, Giraffe!" exclaimed Bumpus, ready to seize upon the idea without stopping to examine the same in order to find out whether or not it were possible to carry it out.

"It ain't half bad," admitted Step Hen.

"But how about starting to sea in this blow?" asked Allan, quietly, after he and Thad had exchanged winks.

"Oh! hang the luck, I clean forgot all about that!" admitted the tall scout, his smile of triumph disappearing immediately.

"Whew! I should say we couldn't!" Bumpus hastened to add, showing that it was possible for a boy to change his opinion almost as speedily as a shift of wind causes the weather vane to turn around, and point toward a new quarter.

"And," added Thad, "that will all have to be left to the morning, anyway. If we should find a half-way chance to do something along those lines, why, we'll gladly give Giraffe the credit for thinking up the scheme. But it's time we settled down for the night now; so let's fix our blankets and be as comfy as we can, even if we do expect to keep awake."

"And don't you think it'd be a good plan, Thad," suggested Step Hen, "to always keep that gun in evidence? If we could make them believe we all of us carried the same kind of weapons, we'd be more apt to see sun-up without any trouble happening; and that's what I think."

"Well, now, there's some meat in that idea of yours, Step Hen," the scout-master told him; "and it wouldn't be a bad scheme for those who have clubs, to carry them more or less this way under your arm, just as you would your gun if tramping, or on a hunt. In the firelight they may think that's what they are, and the effect will be worth something to us, as you say."

All of the boys started to settling down. Policy might have told them that if they made themselves too comfortable the chances of their remaining awake were rather slim.

Bumpus was a lad of good resolutions. No doubt he meant to stay awake just as firmly as Thad himself could have done. But sleeping was one of the fat boy's weak points, and it was not long before he found himself nodding.

Twice he was jabbed in the leg with the point of a pin, once by Giraffe, and the second time by Davy; for the other boys, took his request literally, and doubtless enjoyed having the chance to "do him a to favor."

Each time he was thus punctured the fat scout would start up hurriedly, and open his mouth to give a yell, perhaps under the impression that he had been bitten by a snake, which reptiles he despised, and feared very much.

Discovering where he was in time, however, he had managed to hold his tongue, and muttered to himself that they "needn't go it quite so strong," as he ruefully rubbed his limb where the pin had entered.

After each sudden awakening Bumpus would sit sternly up straight, as though he had taken a solemn vow not to be caught napping again; but as the minutes dragged along he would begin to sink lower and lower again, for sleep was once more getting a firm grip upon him.

When the fat boy reeled for a third time Thad, who was watching operations with more or less amusement, noticed that neither Step Hen nor Davy offered to make any use of their pins; the truth being that both of them had meanwhile gone fast asleep, and hence there were all three in the same boat.

It happened that Bumpus managed to arouse himself presently with a start; as if a sudden consciousness had come upon him. Perhaps he imagined he felt another jab with a pin, and the sensation electrified him.

First he looked on one side and then on the other. When he discovered that his persecutors were both sound asleep, a wide grin came over the good-natured red face of the stout youth. Thad could see him industriously hunting along the lapels of his khaki jacket, as if for a weapon in the shape of a pin; and having secured what he wanted Bumpus carefully reached out both hands, one toward Step Hen and the other in the direction of Davy Jones.

Then, with a low squeal of delight, he gave an outward motion with each hand. There instantly broke forth a chorus of yells that could be heard above the noise of the breakers on the rocks, and the wind rattling the branches of the low oak trees.

"Tit for tat," exclaimed. Bumpus; "what's sauce for the goose is sauce for the gander. After this we'll call it off, fellows, remember. It was give and take, and now the slate's wiped clean."

Davy Jones and Step Hen, quite tired out from their exertions, slept peacefully, one on either side of Bumpus; while Giraffe dozed, and whenever he happened to arouse himself he would wave that hatchet vigorously, as if to call attention to the fact that he was "on deck," and doing full duty.

The long night dragged on.

Once Thad had some good news to communicate.

"Clouds seem to be getting lighter," he announced, pointing overhead.

"Yes," added the other, "and there's a sure enough break, I reckon, p'raps now we'll see something of that old moon before the peep of day comes."

At any rate the fact of the khaki-clad denizens of the camp under the ledge being constantly on guard must have impressed itself upon the minds of the poachers, for they made no hostile move while darkness held sway.

Of course though, both sentries were glad to see the first peep of dawn in the far east. The wind had died down, and there seemed to be some chance that the wild waves would subside by noon, at least sufficiently to allow them to go forth if by any good luck they were given the opportunity to leave the island upon which they had been marooned by so strange a freak of fate.

The others were soon aroused, and made out to have just allowed themselves a few winks of sleep toward morning, though they cast suspicious looks toward each other, Thad noticed. However, neither he nor Allen said a word about the hours that they had been by themselves on guard. The dreaded night had passed, and nothing out of the way had happened, so what was the use of rubbing it in, and making some of their good chums feel badly.

"I think it would be possible to see the place where we left our boat, if I went out on that point there," Thad remarked, while some of the rest were busying themselves in getting breakfast ready, as though meaning to make all the amends possible for their lack of sentry duty.

As though he wished to make sure concerning this matter the scout-master left them, and made his way to the lookout he had indicated. He came back later on, and his face did not seem to show any signs of good news.

"No boat in sight, I take it, Thad?" asked Giraffe, rightly interpreting his lack of enthusiasm.

"It's sure enough gone, and look as hard as I could there didn't seem to be the first sign of the poor Chippeway Belle. Dr. Hobbs' friend will have to buy him another cruising boat, that's sure," Thad told them.

"Well, he can do that, all right, out of the insurance money he collects from that old tub," declared Giraffe, indignantly. "Let me tell you he's been hoping we might sink the thing, somehow or other."

Breakfast was a bountiful meal, because Giraffe happened to be a fellow who disdained half-way measures, when it came to feeding time. The idea of going around half starved so long as there was the smallest amount of food in camp did not suit him at all.

So they ate until every one, even Giraffe, announced that he had had enough; but by that time the frying-pans were empty, and the coffee-pot ditto, so perhaps it may have been this condition of things that influenced some of them to confess to being filled.

The face of the tall boy had become clouded more or less, and it was evident to the scout leader that Giraffe was busily engaged in pondering over something that did not look just right to him.

"What's the matter, Giraffe?" he asked, as they lounged around, enjoying the fire, because the morning had opened quite cool after the blow of the previous night.

"I don't like this thing of an empty pantry, that's what!" observed the other, who could not forget that in less than five hours there was bound to be a demand from somewhere inside that he get busy, and supply another ration; and where was he to get the material to carry out this injunction when their supplies were practically exhausted.

"Well, we can't do anything about it, can we?" demanded Step Hen, trembling in the hopes that the tall scout might have thought of a plan.

"That's just like some fellows," remarked Giraffe, disdainfully; "ready to throw up the sponge at the first show of trouble. Now, I ain 't built that way; and say, I've thought up a plan by which we might get some grub."

"Yes, what might it be?" asked Thad, seeing that the other was waiting for a little encouragement before bursting out into a display of confidence; for he knew Giraffe's ways to a fraction.

"I tell you what we ought to do," the other suddenly explained; "march on that cabin in a bunch, looking mighty determined, and then demand that they supply us with what grub we need to tide us over. There you are; and how about it?"

CHAPTER XXIII

WHERE WAS BUMPUS

"Huh? I don't all speak at once, please. Seems like my splendid idea ain't made a hit like I expected it would. What ails you all?" Giraffe demanded, after a dead silence had fallen upon the little party, instead of the quick response he had hoped for.

"We're waiting to hear from Thad," explained Step Hen, as though he might himself be "up in the air," or, as he would himself have said, "straddling the fence," not knowing whether to scoff at the other's scheme, or give it his unqualified approval.

"Well, I wanted to figure it over in my own mind first," remarked the scout-master, slowly. "It has some good points, Giraffe, but we'll have to get good and hungry before we start to holding up other people and demanding that they supply our wants, even if they are only fish poachers."

"Then you don't think we had ought to rush the cabin, as yet?" asked the other in a disappointed lone.

"Wait awhile; and see what turns up," Thad told him.

"But what could come along to give us a meal around noon?" Giraffe flashed up, always thinking of the main chance, which meant looking after the demands of that voracious appetite.

"Oh! lots of things," laughed Thad. "You know yourself it's the unexpected that keeps happening with us right along. Many a time in the past we didn't have any idea of what was going to stir us up, till it came along. Just now it strikes me all of us ought to stick together, and not go wandering around by ourselves."

"Bumpus ought to be here to get that advice, then," remarked Davy.

At that Thad turned upon the other scout.

"Why, I hadn't noticed that he was away," he said, hastily, and frowning at the same time; "when and where did he go, can you tell me that, Davy, since you seem to be the only one who knows about his being gone?"

"Why, you see, Thad," began the other, looking a trifle alarmed himself now, "he just remembered after we'd had our breakfast, you know, that he must have dropped his belt somewhere; and as he remembered having the same after he came out of the water, he said he expected he'd be able to pick it up between here and that place; so he strolled off. Why, I never thought but what some of the rest of you saw him go; and because nobody said a word I 'spected it was all right."

"How long ago was that, did you say, Davy?" Thad asked.

"Why, just after Giraffe here cleaned out the last piece of bacon in the pan, as he said it was silly to waste even little things; and, after all, he wasted it in a hurry, too, let me tell you," Davy proceeded to say.

"Why, I think that must have been nearly twenty-five minutes ago!" exclaimed Step Hen, in some excitement, as he cast an anxious look away across the rocks and brush that interfered somewhat with their view of the route Bumpus would be apt to take on his way toward their landing place.

Thad jumped to his feet.

"This must be looked into!" he said, decisively.

"You're going off to hunt for him, I take it?" observed Giraffe; "how about not getting separated, like you just told us? Ain't it going from bad to worse, Thad, if so be you rush out by yourself and leave us here?"

"Yes," added Davy, quickly, "if they're alooking around for chances to gobble us up, one by one, first it'd be Bumpus, then our scout-master, and then another of the bunch, till we all got caught. Thad, hadn't we ought to go along with you—"

"Just what I would have proposed, if you'd let me speak," the other assured them readily enough; "so get, ready now, and we'll start off."

"But how about all our stuff here; shall we leave it behind?" questioned Davy.

"Oh! I hope not," remarked Step Hen; "I've got somewhat attached to that blanket of mine, you know."

"Yes, we've noticed that lots of times, when you hated to get up in the morning," chuckled Giraffe.

"But how about it, Thad; do we leave 'em here, and run the chance of getting the same took; or shall we take the stuff along with us?"

"I don't believe these men will bother with such small things as blankets and cooking things; if we had a supply of eatables it might be a different matter; but we happen to be shy along that line. Yes, bundle them up, and hide them 'as best you can. We may be in for a fight, for all we know, and in that case we'd want the freedom of our arms to work those clubs."

"Sounds like business, anyway!" muttered Giraffe, as he started in to do as the scout-master recommended; for obedience is one of the first principles laid down in the rules by which Boy Scout are guided when they subscribe to the regulations of the troop they have joined.

115

They were soon ready.

As the five lads went forth they presented quite a formidable appearance indeed, what with the gun, the camp hatchet, the long bread knife, and a pair of clubs thick enough to give a fellow a nasty headache if ever they were brought in contact with his cranium.

"First of all, it's only right we should give a hail; and if Bumpus is wandering around somewhere he may answer us; and then we can wait for him to come in. I see he's left his bugle with his blanket here; pick it up somebody and give the recall, if anybody knows how."

"Trust that to me!" exclaimed Davy; and snatching up the nickeled instrument he placed it to his lips, immediately sending forth the strident sounds that have done duty on many a battlefield.

No sooner had the last note pealed forth than every boy listened eagerly; but there was no reply.

"Sure he could have heard that, even if he was at the other end of the island," remarked Davy, ready to try again if the scout-master told him to do so.

"And Bumpus has got a good pair of lungs, so he'd be able to let us know he was on to the job, if he had the use of his mouth!" remarked Giraffe, darkly.

"But you don't hear even a peep, do you, fellows?" remarked Step Hen.

"Come on, and fetch that bugle with you, Davy," said Thad; "we might need it again later, you know. I wonder, now, what the poachers will think when they hear a bugle sound? If they don't know anything about the Scouts, they'll think more than ever that we belong to the Canadian militia."

Thad could understand just what course Bumpus was likely to take in passing along the rough surface of the ground between their landing place and the spot where they had found the friendly ledge.

That was the way he expected to go also, keeping constantly on the lookout for any sign calculated to tell him if the fat scout had fallen into difficulties.

It led them down near the edge of the water, too; and this gave Thad a sudden bad feeling. Could it be possible that Bumpus, who was always a clumsy fellow at best, owing to his great bulk, had tripped, and taken a nasty fall, so that his head had struck some cruel rock?

He would not say anything to the rest just now upon that score; but all the same it troubled him not a little as he wandered along, keeping on the alert for just such a trap, into which the missing scout may have fallen.

All at once Thad stopped, and the others saw a peculiar look cross his face. It seemed to tell them that their guide had conceived an idea.

"Guessed where he's gone, have you, Thad?" inquired Giraffe, quickly.

"Well, no, hardly that," was the reply; "but I ought to tell you that right now we're close to that clump of brush that hides the little rock hollow where they've got their boat hidden."

"Oh! mebbe Bumpus he went and took a look in there, just the same as you did, and discovered the boat, too!" remarked Step Hen.

"Well, what if he did, would that explain his absence one little bit?" demanded Davy. "You don't think, now, I hope, our chum is such an idiot that he'd start to take a little cruise out there on that rough water all by himself? Bumpus ain't quite so much in love with sailing as all that, let me tell you right now."

In another minute they were looking at the boat that lay concealed in among the rocks and brush. Thad even jumped down, and passed into its cabin; while the others listened, and waited with their hearts apparently ready to jump up into their throats, lest they caught sounds of a conflict.

But presently the scout-master again appeared, and joined them.

"Not there, then?" asked Giraffe, in a disappointed tone.

"No, but I saw the print of his shoe on the seat of the boat, which shows Bumpus did climb down here; but it was heading outward, so it seems he came up again. Now to look a little further, and find out if he went on toward the spot where we came to land."

They started off, leaving the vicinity of the fish poachers' hidden boat. For a couple of minutes, Thad seemed to be having little or no trouble in following the marks which Bumpus had left behind him; for the fat scout never so much as dreamed that there was such a thing as covering his trail; nor would he have known of any reason for doing anything like this had he been so far up in woodcraft.

"Hold up!" they heard Thad say, suddenly, as he bent over more than he had been doing up to now.

All of the others waited anxiously to hear what the scout-master believed he had discovered, for they could see him moving this way and that. Finally Thad looked up, to disclose a frown upon his usually calm brow.

"Well, would you, believe it," he went on to say, as free from anger as he possibly could bring himself to speak, "they've gone and done it, after all."

"What, Thad?" asked Giraffe, who had been actually holding his breath the while.

"Jumped on our chum right here, and made him a prisoner," came the staggering reply; "I reckon they must have done something rough to him, or we'd have heard him make some kind of an outcry; but they got Bumpus, all right, boys!"

CHAPTER XXIV

LOYAL SCOUTS TO THE RESCUE

This assertion on the part of their leader was so tremendous that for almost a dozen seconds the boys could not utter a single word; but just stood there, and gazed at Thad, speechless.

But it is a very difficult thing to muzzle some lads for any length of time; and Giraffe presently burst out with:

"Jumped on poor Bumpus right here, did they, Thad? And p'raps pounded him into a condition where he just couldn't give the alarm, no matter how hard he tried? Oh! mebbe I don't wish I could have been there to touch up the scoundrels with this fine hatchet? What I'd a done to 'em would have been a caution, let me warn you! But how do you tell all this from the signs, Thad? We're only a bunch of next door to tenderfeet scouts when it comes to reading trail talk; but we know enough to understand when she's explained to us. Please open up, and tell us now."

"And then we must decide what we'll do, so as to rescue our chum," said Step Hen angrily; "because scouts always stand by each other, you know, through thick and thin; and Bumpus is the best fellow agoing, you bear me saying that?"

"Well, it's this way," said the scout-master, always ready to oblige his mates whenever he could do so; "you can see that some sort of a scuffle has taken place where we're standing right now. Other feet than those of Bumpus are marked; and then they all start away from here, heading in that direction. But although Bumpus walked to this spot there's never a sign of his footprints, which I know so well leading off from here."

"What's the answer to that?" asked Davy.

"Why," broke in Giraffe, quickly, "that's as plain as the nose on your face, Davy. Our chum was carried away! Either he couldn't walk because he'd been tapped on the head, and was senseless; or else they had got him tied up that quick."

"Is that so, Thad?" demanded Step Hem

"Giraffe has got the answer all right," came the reply. "I can see where these fellows must have been hiding, and let Bumpus pass them by. Then one dropped down on top of him, so that he couldn't so much as draw in his breath before they had him. This is what I was thinking about when I said we shouldn't be caught off our guard; and that we'd be foolish if we separated at all, for they could pick us off one by one, where they'd be afraid to tackle the whole bunch. It came quicker than I thought it would, though."

"Well, we ain't going to stand for this, I hope?" remarked Giraffe.

"We'd be a fine lot of scouts, wouldn't we," broke in Davy, indignantly, "if we were ready to desert our chum when he was in hard luck? Anybody that knows what the boys of the Silver Fox Patrol of Cranford Troop are would make certain that could never go down with them. Sure we ain't ameaning to keep on hiding our light under a bushel, and sneaking off, while Bumpus, good old Bumpus, is in the hands of the enemy, and p'raps with a splitting headache in the bargain."

"Headache!" echoed Step Hen; "just wait till we get our chance, and if they ain't the fashion among these here poachers, then I don't know beans, and I think I do. Wow! you hear me talking, fellows!" and he caused his club to fairly whistle through the air, as though getting into the swing, so that he would know just how to go about laying out one of the law-breakers when they finally rounded them up.

"Hope we ain't meaning to waste any more time around here than's necessary, Mr. Scout-master?" Giraffe observed, grimly, running his finger suggestively along the edge of the camp hatchet, which they kept in pretty good condition, so that it would really cut quite well.

"We're off right away," said the other.

"And Thad," observed Allan, speaking for the first time, because he was usually a boy of few words, and one who left it to some of the others to do pretty much all the talking, "the new trail, where we fail to find any mark of Bumpus' shoes leads this way, which I take it is toward that shack you said you'd seen last night when you took that little scout on the sly?"

"It sure does, Allan," came the reply.

"Well, then, we must expect that was where they carried our chum; and so we'll make for the cabin now," Allan continued.

"We'll see it soon enough," Thad told them, "because it's only a little ways from where they have their powerboat hidden. Move along as still as you can, boys; and no more talking now—except in whispers."

Every scout must have felt his heart beating like a trip-hammer as the forward progress was continued. The very atmosphere around them seemed to be charged with electricity; at least one would imagine so to see the way they looked suddenly from right to left with quick movements, as they went stooping along.

It was only a space of sixty seconds or so when Thad came to a stop. They knew from this that the cabin spoken of must already have been sighted;

and this proved to be the case, as was made apparent when they came to examine the territory just ahead.

Among the rocks and undergrowth it could hardly be seen; indeed, if they had not known of its presence there, possibly none of them would have thought a cabin was so near by.

They stared hard at it, but failed to see the first sign of any living being in the neighborhood.

"Any signs of 'em, Thad?" whispered Giraffe, who was close at the heels of the scout-master; so close indeed, that Thad had more than once wondered whether the tall and nervous scout were still waving that up-to-date tomahawk, and if he the leader, might be so unlucky as to get in the way of the dangerous weapon.

"Nothing that I can see," Thad answered, softly.

"But you think they're in that place, don't you?" Giraffe continued to ask.

"Like as not they are," the scout-master replied.

All of them were staring hard at what they now saw. Having continued to advance a little farther they made out what seemed to be a lot of barrels; and some of them must have contained ice, to judge from the straw scattered about. Well, ice was needed in order to properly pack fish for the market; and if the poachers had ever had a supply on the island, secured during the winter time, it must have been exhausted before now, because the season was late.

Yes, and what was more to the point, as the breeze happened to waft an odor to their noses all of the scouts detected the strong and unmistakable smell of fish, which must always be associated with every fishing camp.

"Are we agoing to walk straight up to that door, and knock it in?" asked Giraffe, after they had stood there for a couple of anxious minutes, staring hard at the lone shack, as though trying to peer through the log walls, and see what lay within.

"That might be hardly the thing for scouts to do," Thad told him. "They are taught to be cautious as well as brave. If those men happen to be hiding inside there, wouldn't they have a fine chance to riddle us if we walked right up as big, as camels? No, we've got to show a little strategy in this thing, eh, Allan?"

"Just what we have, Mr. Scout-master."

"So let's begin by circling around, and coming up on the shack from the other side," Thad said this he started off, with the others skulking along behind, about like a comet is followed by its tail.

They kept a bright lookout all the while, not meaning to let the poachers get the better of them by creeping away from the shack while the boys in khaki were carrying out this evolution. Nothing however was seen. If the men were still in there they kept very quiet, everybody thought; and somehow this worried more than one of the scouts.

Giraffe could not see what all this creeping around was intended for, anyhow; he would have been in favor of separating, and rushing toward the cabin from as many points of the compass as there were scouts. That sort of plan at least had the benefit of speed; for they would either be at the door inside of ten seconds, or have been staggered with a volley from within.

But it would not be for much longer, because even now they had made such good progress that a few minutes more must put them through.

It seemed an age to Giraffe since they had started to creep to the other side of the shack; when he saw by the actions of their leader that Thad was now ready to order the real advance.

There did not appear to be any sign of a window on this side of the rude building, so that the chances were no one inside could watch their coming; which Giraffe well knew had been the principal reason why Thad had chosen to make this rear approach.

"Now listen, all of you," whispered the leader, in thrilling tones; "I'm going to call out to Bumpus, and perhaps we'll get a clue regarding what's happened to him."

Raising his voice, he called out the name of the fat scout twice in succession, being very particular to speak it distinctly, so that any one within would have to be absolutely deaf not to hear it.

There was no reply, that is, nothing in the way of an answering voice; but all of them caught a peculiar sound that kept up intermittently for almost a full minute.

"Now, what sort of a queer rumpus would you call that?" asked Step Hen.

"Made me think of somebody kicking his heels into the floor, or some such stunt as that," Giraffe declared; while Davy nodded his head, as though there was no need for him to say anything when another voiced his sentiments so exactly.

"Thad, are we going to stand this any longer?" Allan demanded,

122

"No, we must see what's inside that place; so come along, boys, and we'll break in the door!" with which words the scout-master ran quickly forward, the others almost outstripping him, so great was their eagerness to be "in the swim," no matter what happened.

The door seemed to be fastened in some way; though there was nothing in the way of a pistol shot or even a gruff voice warning them off.

Thad tried in vain to find the fastening.

"Pick up that log, and use it as a battering ram!" he ordered; and the other four scouts hastened to do so, while the patrol leader stood ready with his gun, not knowing how soon he might have need of it for defense.

As the log came crashing against the door it flew wide open, proving that it had never been really intended as a means for keeping enemies out. Dropping the log, and at once snatching up their weapons, the scouts rushed to the open doorway, to stare into the cabin. What they saw amazed, and yet delighted them. There was not an enemy in sight; but some object moved upon the hard puncheon floor; and looking closer they discovered that it was no other than Bumpus, bound hand and foot, gagged, and with his face as red as a boiled lobster, redder by far than his fiery hair.

CHAPTER XXV

NOT SO GREEN AS HE LOOKED

The only reason that Bumpus did not call out help! was because the rough gag, consisting of a cloth tied about the lower part of his face, prevented him from saying a single word.

It was a sight that staggered the other scouts, although at the same time they felt considerable satisfaction at finding their lost chum so speedily, and thus learning that he had not come to very serious harm.

There was an immediate rush made inside the shack, each seeming desirous of being the first to render Bumpus assistance. All but the scoutmaster entered in this promiscuous way, and Thad was too wise a bird to be caught with chaff. What if this should be some sort of a trap, into which the rest of the boys were rushing headlong? He did not stop to consider how they might be caught, but made up his mind that it was policy on his part to stand guard there at the door.

There were more than enough hands to free the prisoner, and he would not be missed in that way. So Thad, handling his ready gun suggestively, and keeping a keen lookout for signs of trouble, stood there, waiting for the rest to come out.

Amidst more or less confusion Bumpus was unbound, after that gag had been removed from his mouth. The first thing he did was to breathe heavily, as though during his confinement he had not been able to get his wind as freely as he liked. Then, when he could get on his feet with the help of Step Hen and Giraffe, he stamped on the cloth that had done duty as a preventative of speech.

"Oh! what haven't I suffered, having that measly old thing under my nose for ages, and this smell of fish everywhere around me!" he exclaimed, as though fairly bursting with indignation. "How long have I been shut up here, anyway, fellows? Seems like days and weeks must a passed since they took me. I kinder lost my senses I reckon, after that chap dropped on top of me, like the mountain was acoming down. Please tell me what day of the week this is?"

At this the others looked puzzled.

"Why, you sure must be locoed, Bumpus, to get so twisted as that!" declared Giraffe.

"I should say he was!" echoed Davy.

"Why, this is the same morning after the storm, don't you know, Bumpus, really and truly it is," Step Hen went on to assert, with a ring of pity in his voice. "And, say, did you think it was to-morrow, or the next day, and we'd just about forgotten we had a chum who was missing? Well, if this don't take the cake, I never heard the beat of it."

"Fetch him outside so I can ask a few questions!" called Thad just then.

"Yes, for goodness sake get me where I can have a whiff of clean air; I'm nearly dead with this fishy smell. I always did hate to handle fish after they got over their jumping stage, and this is awful!" Bumpus wailed.

"It certain is," muttered Giraffe, holding his fingers up to his nose.

So they all bustled out of the door, where they found the scout-master on duty; and all at once it struck the other fellows how smart Thad had been in holding back at the time the rush was made to free Bumpus.

"Oh! this is a thousand per cent better!" the late prisoner declared, with genuine thanksgiving in his tones, as he fairly reveled in the clear air that had been purified by the recent blow.

"I heard you asking what day this was, and from that we understand that you must have lost your senses for a while, and got mixed up?" Thad remarked.

"That's what happened, Thad," replied the other, promptly enough.

"Well, it's not only the same morning after the storm," continued the other, "but just about an hour after you went off to hunt for your belt. I see you found the same, and that they made good use of it to fasten your arms behind your back."

Bumpus looked astonished, as though what he heard was hard to believe; for he shook his head slowly, and observed:

"Tell me about that, will you? Well, sir, that was the longest hour that ever happened to me in all my life!"

"Hold on!" corrected Giraffe, "you're forgetting that time you tripped in the dark, and fell over a precipice a thousand feet deep, and hung there from the top, yelling for help. We came galloping to the spot, and rescued you, about as limp as a dish-rag; and you told us how you'd suffered such agonies that you lived ten years, and wanted to know if your hair had turned white. But when we held the light over the top of that awful precipice, and showed you that the ground was just about six inches below your toes as you dangled there, why, you made out that it was all a good joke, and that anyhow you'd given the rest of us a bad scare."

Bumpus grinned, as though the recollection rather amused him now.

"But this time it was different, Giraffe, because they wanted me to tell, and I just wouldn't. Then the big man who was leader, gave me a knock on the head, he was so mad at me, and I keeled over a second time. That's when I thought days had passed, when I heard you fellows talking outside, and after that an earthquake came knocking down the door. My! but I was glad to see the bunch come piling in, you can take it from me. Never will forget it, I give you my word, boys!"

"But see here, Bumpus," said Thad, "what do you mean when you say you refused to tell? Of course all of us know how stubborn you can be, when you take a notion; but what could these men want to get out of you that you'd refuse to let go? Not any information about us, I should think?"

"Well, hardly," replied the other. "You see, they had me tied up, and that horrible fishy rag fastened around my mouth so I couldn't talk; but the fellow that could speak United States bettern'n either of the others told me to nod my head if I promised to show 'em where I'd hid it; but every time I shook it this way," and he proceeded to give an emphatic demonstration of what a negative shake might be.

"But what had you hid away that they wanted so badly?" persisted Thad.

Bumpus grinned, and raised one of his eyebrows in a comical manner.

"Oh! that was a little trick of mine," he remarked, composedly. "P'raps the rest of you'll give me credit for being a mite smart when I tell you. But in order to make you understand, just wait till I go back to the time I left camp to look for this belt."

"That's the best way, I should think," agreed Giraffe, who knew from experience how hard it sometimes proved to drag the details of a story from Bumpus.

"Oh! I ain't meaning to string it out everlastingly!" declared the other. "I'm going to be right to the point, see if I don't. Well, after I picked up my belt I just happened to remember what Thad had told us about that concealed boat belonging to the queer chaps who were hiding on this island; and before I knew hardly what I was doing I found myself aboard the same, nosing around.

"All at once it struck me what a bad job for us it'd be if they took a notion to skip out after the wind and waves went down, and left us here by our lonely. So I made up a cute little plan calculated to block that game right in the start. What did I do? Just unfastened the crank they used to start the engine agoing and hid the same under my coat. I was meaning to fetch it to our camp, so we could make terms with the men, when I thought I saw somebody slip around a tree and, on the impulse of the moment, as they say in the books, I just let that handle drop into the hollow of a stump I happened to be passing."

"Good for you, Bumpus!" exclaimed Giraffe, patting the other on the shoulder.

"Well, it wasn't so very good for me in one way," the fat scout remarked, with one hand tenderly caressing a bump he seemed to have on his head; "because that same little trick got a fellow of my size in heaps of trouble right away. But you know how I hate to give a thing up, boys; and once I'd done this job I was bent on holding out to the bitter end.

"Well, to make a long story short, the next thing I knew I didn't know anything, because that big clodhopper came down from a tree right on top of me, and one of his shoes must a struck me on the head right here, for it hurts like the mischief.

"When I came to my senses I was fixed up like you saw, and inside this old fish house. Honest boys, first thing, before I got a good look around, I thought I had died, and was amouldering in my grave. The three men were hanging over me, ajabbering like so many monkeys or poll parrots. Then the big fellow with the black beard began to throw all sorts of questions at me, which I managed to understand.

"Seems like they had gone to the boat after leaving me here, p'raps meaning to take chances out on the lake, waves or no waves, because they thought if they stayed any longer they were agoing to be gobbled by the soldiers, sure pop. And then they missed that old crank. Course they knowed I'd been pottering around their boat, and they wanted to find out what I did with the handle, because it happens you can't start that engine like some I've seen, in an emergency, without the crank.

"We had it pretty warm back and forth for a session, him a firing questions at me, sometimes in French, and again in mixed English; and me a shaking my head right and left to tell him I wouldn't give up the information, not if he kept going for a coon's age. And sudden like, he got so fiery mad he just slapped me over the head, and I admit I lost all interest in things on this same earth till I came to, and heard voices outside that seemed familiar like. You know the rest, boys; now let's get away from this place in a hurry. I'll taste rank fish for a month of Sundays, sure I will. Ugh!"

"Wait, don't be in such a hurry, Bumpus," said Thad. "First of all I want to say that you've done a smart thing, even if it was reckless; because with that boat in our hands we can really leave Sturgeon Island any time we want,

127

once the lake quiets down some. And on the way back to camp we'll just pick up that crank, after which all we have to do is to make sure these three frightened men don't jump in on us, and take us by surprise. But while we're here we ought to see what they've got that makes them want to avoid the officers who patrol the lakes looking for smugglers, game-fish poachers and the like."

"Give me the gun then, Thad," said Allan, promptly, as he saw the other glance toward him; "and I'll stay out here on guard while some of the rest investigate."

"Thanks, that pleases me," replied the scout-master, relinquishing the weapon that had proved to be worth its weight in silver to them, in that it cowed the trio of lawless men who had their headquarters on Sturgeon Island.

CHAPTER XXVI

THE SKIES BEGIN TO BRIGHTEN

It was not very light inside the cabin, so that the first thing Thad did in his customary energetic way was to take a lantern from a hook, and put a match to the wick. After that they could see better.

"Don't seem, to be much of anything around here now that we can see halfway decent," remarked Giraffe.

"Oh I ain't there?" said Bumpus, who was, pinching his nose between his thumb and forefinger, "now, it strikes me there's a whole lot, when you come to think."

"However those men could sleep in here beats me?" ejaculated Step Hen, who was not looking very happy himself, as he sniffed around.

"Oh! mebbe you'll kinder get a little used to it after awhile," Bumpus assured him, in a tone meant to be comforting.

"I don't believe they did sleep in here at all," Thad remarked, after he had been spying around a little longer. "You can't see a sign of a bed, or a blanket, or even leaves in a corner to tell where anybody laid down."

"And outside of these few old oilskin rags that they use to wear in their business," added Giraffe, "and hung up on nails along this wall, there ain't anything to tell that they stayed here. Say, Thad, whatever do you think this shack could a been used for?"

"Where's your nose?" demanded Bumpus at that juncture.

"Yes," Thad went on to say, "that's about the only thing you need to tell you, Giraffe. Seems like they must store their catch here until they get enough on hand to pay to stop work, and pack and ship the same out. Let's look around. What d'ye call this but a kind of trap in the floor?"

"It sure is, Thad," admitted the tall scout, promptly.

"Looks like it had been used a heap, in the bargain," advanced Step Hen.

"Why, of course, because there must be some sort of well underneath the house, where they keep ice all the while, and drop the fish in as they net them. Perhaps one reason why they hate to leave here in a rush is that they've got illegal nets out in different places right now, which cost a heap of money, and they hate to let them go. Hand me that strip of iron, please, Davy. Looks to me as if they use this to pry up the trap. There, what did I tell you?"

As the scout-master said this he managed to skillfully raise the square that was cut in the floor of the cabin. Underneath the old building there must have been a natural well in among the rocks; for as Thad held the lantern over so that all of the boys could see, they discovered what looked like a cellar of solid stone, some fifteen feet deep, and with a ladder at one side that was doubtless used as a means of passing up and down.

"Well! I declare! look at the piles of fine fish, will you?" exclaimed

Step Hen.

"All sorts too—trout, white fish, and even black bass, whoppers at that!" added Davy, staring at such a remarkable sight.

"They must take these in some way that's against the law!" Thad declared. "Their suspicious actions prove that, plain enough."

"That's the greatest lot of game fish I ever saw together!" Giraffe ventured, "and if such things keep going on, chances are even the Great Lakes'll be drained of decent sport before many years. It's a shame, that's what it is."

Bumpus was the only one who had made no remark; but all the same he seemed to be busy. They saw him dive into a pocket, and what should he fetch out brut a stout fish line wound around a bobbin, and with a hook attached. This he immediately began unrolling so that the end carrying hook and sinker fell down toward the bottom of the pit.

"Look at Bumpus, would you?" exclaimed Step Hen; "he's gone clean dippy, that's what? Thinks he's out on the lake, and these fish are swimming down there waitin' to bite at his bait! Poor old Bumpus, that knock on the head was too much for him!"

"Was, hey?" snapped the object of this commiseration, as he went on unreeling his line; "you just wait and see whether I've lost my mind, or if I ain't as bright as a button. See that buster of a trout alying there on top? Well, that beats the record so far; and if I can only tip my hook under his gill I'm meaning to yank him up here the quickest you ever saw. Guess the rules and regulations of our watch only said a fellow had to catch his fish with hook and line; it never told that they had to be alive, and swimming, not a word of it. You watch me win that championship right here!"

"There's a fish pile down in the cellar," spoke up the rival of Bumpus, indignantly, "and what d'ye think, Bumpus here means to fetch up a lot of 'em with his hook and line, and count the same against me. Hey! guess two can play at that sort of game, if there's going to be anything in it; so look out; because I'm after that same big trout myself."

Twice Bumpus managed to get his hook where it seemed to catch upon the monster trout's exposed gill, and with a cry of triumph he started to pull in; but on one occasion the slender hold his hook had taken broke away; and the second time it chanced that Giraffe had managed to fasten his barb somewhere about the dorsal fin of the fish, so that there was an immediate struggle for supremacy, with the usual result in such cases that the anticipated prize fell back, and was lost to both contestants.

"Tell them to let up on that silly business, and let's get out of here, Thad," said Step Hen, when this thing had gone on for some time, with no result save a weariness to the two rivals.

"But seems to me," Dave put in just then, "that couple of them same trout and white fish would be mighty tasty dish for a bunch of scouts I know of who always carry their appetites with them."

When Giraffe heard him say that, he suddenly seemed to lose all his fierceness as a contestant for honors.

"Here, let's stop this business, Bumpus, because I ain't agoing to let you grab up any fish that easy like; and I reckon you feel the same way about me. Anyhow, I leave it to Thad here if it's a sportsmanlike way of scoring in our game? If he says no, why I'm willing to let you hook up some of the beauties for our dinner; or to make things more lively I agree to climb down that greasy old ladder and put 'em on the hook for you. How about it, Mr. Scout-master; is it fair?"

"Perhaps the letter of the law might favor such a course," he said, solemnly; "but we pretend to be sportsmen, all of us, and as such we go farther than that. And Bumpus, you know very well that nothing of this kind was thought of when you made your wager with Giraffe. As I was counted on to be the umpire I say now and here that the fish taken have to be alive at the time they are hooked, and swimming in the lake."

"Then that settles it, Thad," chuckled Bumpus, with a grin; "anyhow, I was only fooling, and wouldn't want to count honors won so cheap as this. But drop down there, Giraffe, since you were so kind as to promise, and hook me on that gay fellow I nearly had two different times. Let me feel how heavy he is? I'd go myself, but chances are I'd sure collapse down there, because already I'm feeling weak again, and that's the truth."

Giraffe evidently did not mean to go back on his word; and accordingly he carefully climbed over the edge of the opening, found a resting place for his feet on the top round of the ladder, and then began to slowly descend.

First of all he hooked on the big trout, and gaily Bumpus pulled the prize up, remarking at the time that it felt as though he were lifting a grindstone.

When he lowered his line again Giraffe had a splendid fresh looking white fish ready, and this he sent up, after the trout.

"I just can't stand this any longer," the boy below called up; "and I'm acomin' right along with the next one, which ought to be a white fish, I reckon. Oh! my! hope I don't keel over before I get to the top. If I do, please, please don't run away and leave me to my fate, boys!"

Perhaps Giraffe was only joking, but it was noticed that when he hastily clambered out of the fish pit he made a streak for outdoors, still hanging on to his latest capture.

In fact, as they had had enough of that thing, all of them hastened to follow the example set by the tall and lanky scout. Outside they found Allan examining the prize with considerable interest, while Giraffe was fanning himself, and making all sorts of grimaces as he raised first one hand and then the other to his nose.

"I'll step in and take a look now, while we're here," mentioned Allan; "because I may never get another chance to see what a fish poacher's storage place is like."

"Queer where they've gone and hidden themselves," Step Hen remarked, as he looked all around as though half expecting to see a bearded face thrust out of the bushes, or above a pile of rocks near by.

"Well, just now they're in a sort of panic, and hardly know what to try next," Thad told them. "Of course they must see that we're only boys, after all; but from the fact that we wear uniforms they suppose we are connected in some way with the militia, and that perhaps a boatload of soldiers is even now on the way here, obeying some sort of wireless signal we've managed to transmit. They thought to seize Bumpus, and perhaps get us all, one by one; but when they found that he had rendered their boat helpless they just threw up the sponge and quit."

"Well, I kinder feel a mite sorry for the rascals," Step Hen observed; whereupon the usually gentle Bumpus, who could be depended on to forgive the first one of all, fired up, and burst out with:

"Then I ain't, not one whit; and I guess you wouldn't either, Step Hen Bingham, if you had a lump as big as a hickory nut on top of your head, that felt as sore as a boil, and knew one of that crowd did it to you. Ain't they breaking the law of the land; and every fish they take in their illegal nets or seines means one less for the fellow that fishes for sport, or the man that does business according to the rules and regulations. Sorry, well I guess not! And when we move away with their old boat we'll send somebody with brass buttons over to Sturgeon Island to take off the marooners."

"Whew! listen to the savage monster, would you?" purred Step Hen; but Bumpus had suffered too much to be in a forgiving humor, and he continued to shake his head ominously while he kept on breathing out threatenings, like Saul of old.

"Now let's head for our camp," Thad gave the order, when Allan had joined them, and declared he had seen all he wanted of the fish poachers' storehouse.

"I only hope they haven't stolen a march on us, and got away with our traps," Davy happened to remark, as they stepped out at a lively rate.

"What a job we'd have cookin' these fine fish, if we didn't have any frying-pan," was the first lament of Giraffe.

"And my blanket that I think so much of, I wouldn't like to lose that," Bumpus told them; but Thad gave it as his opinion that after the men had fled, upon hearing the voices of the boys near by, they must have fallen into such a panic that no doubt they were now in hiding away off at the other end of the island.

"Now don't forget to show us where you hid that crank belonging to the boat engine, Bumpus," Step, Hen cautioned, as they strode along.

"Good thing you spoke of it when you did, Step Hen," the fat scout declared, "because here's the old stump right now. Feel down, and see if it ain't there, somebody. Here, let me do it myself, because I know just where it lies."

In proof of his words Bumpus speedily drew out the crooked bit of steel in question.

"Here you are, Giraffe, like to like!" he sang out gaily, as he tossed his find toward the tall scout.

"I s'pose that's as much as calling me a crank," muttered Giraffe; "but then, we'd take anything from you, Bumpus, just now, we feel so good after your splendid work."

Of course upon receiving that fine compliment Bumpus became contrite at once.

"Excuse me for saying that, Giraffe," he called out; "because I reckon now you ain't one whit more a crank than some others in this crowd." And then noticing that Step Hen and Davy were looking daggers at him, he hurriedly added, "particularly a stout feller they call Bumpus for short instead of Cornelius Jasper Hawtree."

"My idea is about this," Thad went on to say; "as we are going to depend so much on using this boat to get away in, we'd better make our camp right alongside; and in that way they won't have much chance to steal the same from us."

"But ain't we going away soon?" asked Davy, looking around him again, as though he still expected to see a party of furious poachers rush towards them, reinforcements having meanwhile arrived on the island.

"Not till that sea goes down a whole lot more," replied the scout-master; "and if that doesn't happen until late this afternoon I'm afraid we'll have to spend one more night on Sturgeon Island," which information the others did not hear with any degree of enthusiasm for they were all heartily tired of the place.

CHAPTER XXVII

TAKEN UNAWARES, AFTER ALL

As there was no longer any necessity for their depending upon the shelter of the projecting ledge, since the sun was shining cheerily, the scouts set about changing camp.

This did not take any great while, because they had no tents to bother with; and it was easy enough to gather up their blankets and the few things they had saved from the wreck of the Chippeway Belle.

As none of them ever saw the first sign of that ill-fated boat again, it was always taken for granted that when the wind shifted in the night, at the time Thad drew attention to the fact, the strain became so great that the anchor cable had to give way, allowing the still floating boat to be carried out into deep water before the end came.

They found the anchor where it had been placed, with the rope broken part way out, and this told the story as well as words could have.

And so camp was made close by the boat belonging to the fish poachers, which it must be their duty to guard, so that later on they could make use of the same in order to escape from the island.

The waves did not go down as rapidly as the boys would have liked, and when high noon came they were still rolling along in a way that was dangerous to any small craft, especially on such a great inland sea as Superior is, with harbors few and far between.

Thad admitted that the chances of their getting away that day did not look good to him. Giraffe was the only real cheerful fellow in the party, and as he superintended the cooking of the delicious white fish for lunch he was heard to express his opinion several times.

"Well, one thing good about it is that there's enough fish on the ice down in that well to last us till Christmas; and it's to be hoped that somebody with a boat comes along before then, to take us off; or we can get this chunky craft of the poachers to working some. But let me tell you, that same fish does smell grand to me. Needn't make a face, Bumpus, because you think you'll never eat fish again. It's either that or go hungry with this crowd."

"But the white fish, like all other delicate fish, is only at its best when eaten on the spot where it's caught," Thad told them; "putting it on ice for days hurts the flavor, and sometimes it's just as tasteless as so much sawdust."

135

"Then this one was fresh caught," Giraffe affirmed, as he looked hastily about, took up the last bit that was in the second pan, and asked: "anybody want this; if nobody else does, I'm Johnny on the spot."

"Well, I declare, I like that!" burst out Step Hen; "did you see him swing that pan around, and before a fellow could even open his mouth to say yes, he had that last big piece in his tin dish. Oh! well, since you've got to be filled up, or you get to growling, go ahead and bolt, it; only look out for bones. If one ever got fastened in that rubber neck of yours, Giraffe, nobody's fingers could ever reach it. And as hard luck would have it, I left my fish disgorger at home."

Giraffe never minded this sort of talk, for he was making away with the last of the fish with his usual speed.

"Bones never trouble him at all," remarked Bumpus, who was always telling about dreaming of choking to death on a fish-bone.

"That's where you're wrong," chuckled Step Hen; "they trouble him a whole lot, every time he sits down, I reckon, because Nature ain't been so kind to our long friend as to you, Bumpus."

Joking in this style they finished their meal, and the afternoon stared them in the face. It promised to be a long stretch, if they had to stay there until another morning.

Bumpus and Giraffe presently got their lines out, and finding a place near by where it seemed safe to remain, they started to try and add to their score.

"Let's call it off, Bumpus," suggested Giraffe, who was getting weary. "What's the use of all this bother, when we've got a storehouse cram-full of fine fresh fish close at hand, so we sure don't need this sort of a job for the sake of filling our stomachs. Anyhow, you can keep it up if you feel like it; I'm dead sleepy after passing such a night; and we ought to get some rest."

"That's so," echoed Bumpus, just as if he had been on guard every minute of the previous night, "and as like as not we'll have to be keeping one eye open to-night again, who knows?"

"One?" cried Giraffe, looking sharply at him; and then shaking his head he went on to add: "but I said I wasn't agoing to poke fun at you this whole day, Bumpus, after what you done. Course you can't help it if you get sleepy, any more'n I can about being hungry all the time. So let's call it a draw, and quit kidding."

"What's that smoke over there mean?" asked Step Hen, a short time later; and even Giraffe, who was trying to get some sleep, sat up on hearing this.

"Hurrah! mebbe it's a rescue boat coming out after us!" cried Davy, standing on his hands, and kicking his heels in the air, just as the ordinary boy might clap his hands together.

"What do you say, Thad?" asked Giraffe, cautiously, having arisen to his feet, and stretched his long neck in the endeavor to see better than his chums.

"Well," remarked the scout-master, after he had made a mental calculation; "you notice, don't you, that it comes from toward the other end of the island."

"Yes, that's a fact, Thad," slowly admitted Davy, who had now returned to his normal condition, with his head higher than his heels; though some of the boys often declared that the reverse was true, and that he seemed more natural when hanging head downward from the limb of a tree, like a giant bat or a monkey.

"And there isn't enough of it to make me think a boat could be coming," Thad went on to say. "In fact, the chances are those men, as badly frightened as they are, have to eat, and I think they've lighted a fire to cook something."

"Oh! is that all?" grunted Giraffe, immediately dropping back upon his blanket; "please don't wake me up again for such a silly thing as that; though of course I can feel for 'em if they are really hungry."

Acting on the advice of Thad the other boys managed to get some sleep from time to time, though they were very careful not to let the camp go unguarded.

"We're going to be kept here on the island another night, seems like," he had told them, "and that means a constant watch. So far we've managed to hold our own, and we can't afford to get careless, and lose out."

"I should say not," Step Hen had echoed, as he cuddled down to carry out the suggestion of the scout-master.

Along about half an hour before evening set in an expedition was arranged to pay another friendly visit to the fish preserves of the poachers. They wanted to get enough supplies this time to cover several meals, so that they would be able to feel that they had food for the next day, should they be able to make the start in the morning.

Now Bumpus would much rather have remained behind; but it was a choice between two evils with him. His recollections of the harsh methods by means of which the poachers tried to get him to give up his secret were still fresh in his mind; so was his detestation of that fishy odor that clung to the

137

shack. But Thad would not let him have any choice in the matter, telling him that he must accompany the expedition, and carry home his share of the spoils, though Giraffe had promised to again drop down into the pit, and send up all they wanted.

They met with no adventure on the way, nor were they interrupted in their task of securing a store of fish food for present necessities, and looking into the near future a bit.

Giraffe managed his end of the labor manfully. He suffered a great deal, he admitted; but then, somebody had to take on the hard jobs; and as no one else volunteered he just had to be the "goat."

"Oh! as if we don't know the real reason," Step Hen declared, indignantly. "If you wasn't so crazy after eating all the time, I guess now you'd be the last one to go down there of your own free will. But that ain't saying we ain't glad of it. 'Taint often we get a chance to harness that appetite of yours to something that pays. Go on down a few more times, Giraffe; we might toddle along under another fish apiece."

"Not much I will," grunted the other; "six trips is the limit for anybody with a weak stomach."

"Weak stomach-what, you?" cried Step Hen, scornfully throwing up his hands.

The tall scout however did not want to be drawn into an argument just then, since that would only delay their departure from the cabin and all that it spoke of in such a distinct way. He darted in again, however, for a last visit, and vanished down the pit; to appear a minute later holding the largest fish they had as yet run across.

"There, what d'ye think of that for a jim dandy, fellows?" he cried. "And Bumpus, take a good look at him, because I'm bound to hook the mate to this next time we get out our lines. I'm not only a weather prophet, but there are times when I feel it in my bones that something is going to happen."

He tripped just then, and took a header, whereupon Bumpus, with pretended sympathy, hurried to his side, and offered to help him get up, saying;

"Oh! Giraffe, that was the time your bones told you the truth, didn't they; and I reckon your knee joints are skinned some after that tumble, too?"

Giraffe may have been suffering all sorts of agonies at the time, but of course he was not going to let the others see him wince; so he smiled sweetly as he once more gained his feet, and took up the big fish, saying at the same time:

"Don't mention it; I'm all right, Bumpus."

But they could see him limp more or less as they headed for the camp by the captured motorboat of the fish poachers.

Of course, when they went off like this they made sure to carry the crank belonging to the engine along with them, so that even if the enemy did enter the camp during their absence they could not run away with the craft, which on account of the make of motor was practically helpless as soon as the crank was gone.

"Here we are, right-side up with care; plenty of grub, and no damage done except that we've decreased the stock of fish supplies the poachers have laid by," Step Hen was heard to declare; and though Giraffe gave him a pained look, and unconsciously rubbed his injured knee, he did not make any remark to the contrary.

And when it came time to get supper ready he was apparently just as able to move around as ever, barring a slight limp.

Of course they kept close watch all the while, not wishing to be taken by surprise, should the enemy muster up enough courage to attempt some desperate trick, possibly looking to making the scouts prisoners, so that they could once more secure the valuable crank, and go away on board their boat.

Thad himself had managed to secure some rest during the day, because he knew that another hard night awaited him.

As on the previous occasion he told the others they could sit up if they chose, and keep both he and Allan company; and just as had happened before all of them tried hard to accommodate; but before one hour passed poor Bumpus had fallen by the wayside; and then soon afterward Davy, Giraffe and Step Hen all found themselves unable to hold out.

Since they had really undergone considerable in the way of privation and excitement of late, Thad did not have the heart to blame them. He believed that with the one faithful chum alongside, he could take as good care of the camp as though the whole six were on duty.

The time dragged along until it must have been close on midnight; and so far nothing out of the way had happened, though the sentries did not relax their vigilance on that account, for they were too good woodsmen to think of that.

As the boat had been secured with all the available ropes, and a part of the engine dismantled in the bargain, neither of the scouts dreamed that the enemy would aim to strike a blow at them in that quarter. They could not

139

carry the boat off; and even granting that this were possible, it would be useless, since they had no means for running the same.

Still another hour had crept along, and Thad was just beginning to congratulate himself on the way the night was passing, when without the least, warning there came a sudden flash of light down in the rocky berth where the boat lay; immediately succeeded by a deafening crash. Up into the air arose burning fragments of the poacher's boat; and this was the startling spectacle that greeted the astonished eyes of the Silver Fox scouts who had been sweetly sleeping, as they sat up and stared around them.

CHAPTER XXVIII

GOOD-EYE TO STURGEON ISLAND—CONCLUSION

All sorts of loud cries and exclamations arose, as the startled boys began to dodge the falling pieces of the blown-up boat.

Thad, although almost stunned by the sudden catastrophe that had come upon them, in spite of their vigilance, kept a bright lookout, for fear lest the next thing they knew the poachers would come dashing among them, hoping to take advantage of the confusion to disarm them.

But nothing of the sort occurred, and presently the six boys huddled there in a heap, trying to figure out what had happened, and why the three men had resorted to such desperate tactics rather than allow the seeming soldiers to sail away in the morning, and perhaps carry the news to some place where the authorities would be sure to fit out an expedition at once, looking to their capture.

After a great deal of talk, and many odd ideas being advanced, which it would not profit us to mention here, they settled on what seemed to be the most plausible theory. This was that the three poachers, believing they could not make use of their boat so long as the boys in uniform held the key, in the shape of that crank, had decided to blow it up. Their reason for this may have been that they would in this way compel the others to remain marooned there on the island; and perhaps it was expected that another boat, with a fresh lot of poachers, would be along after a certain time.

This was the nearest they could ever come to it, for they did not have a chance to make the personal acquaintance of the three hide-out men, and therefore could not get information at first quarters.

When the morning came the scouts were not so merry as they had felt on the previous evening when all things looked rather rosy. Still, it is difficult to keep some fellows moping all the time; and even Giraffe tried hard to look at the bright side; thought he often complained that he had consider difficulty in making up his mind which side that was.

As long as the food supply held out, Giraffe was not going to give up to despair; even if fish as a steady diet might pall on the ordinary appetite, Giraffe thought he could stand the bill of fare for a week or two, if they had to stick it out that long.

Thad kept them on the watch for some sort of vessel, steamer, sailing craft, whaleboat barge or anything that would afford an asylum, if only they could by the greatest of good luck attract the attention of those on board.

141

As the morning got pretty well along the boys were beginning to feel downcast once more, when all at once Step Hen, who had been using the glasses at the time, let out a joyous whoop.

"Would you believe it, fellows," he cried, "while we've been nearly breaking our necks looking to the east and south for a sail, why, here's a little buzzing motorboat acoming along an the same tack we carried; and ten chances to one now, it's carrying our two good Silver Fox pards, Smithy and Bob White!"

All of them had to take a look through the glasses, and the consensus of opinion seemed to trend that way; though at first some of the more dubious were inclined to fear that it might only be another poaching boat, that was coming straight to the island to land a catch of illegally taken fish.

"Get busy right away, and let them know where we are!" exclaimed Bumpus, all of a tremble with anxiety. "Goodness gracious! just think how we'd feel if they went speeding past old Sturgeon Island, never heating us yell; because the breeze was wrong. Bang away with the gun, Thad, and make 'em look! Do something that'll stir things up! Wish I could let out a whoop that'd carry ten miles, you'd hear me spreading myself some, I tell you."

But all Bumpus's fears were useless, for those aboard the little motorboat that had really come all the way from the Soo, starting earlier than Thad and his five companions, heard the combined shouts, and signaled that they would head in without delay.

"Say, couldn't you hold up a little while, and let me go back after a few more of those fine fish?" pleaded Giraffe, when the rescuing craft was drawing close; and when the scout-master shook his head in the negative the tall member went on: "you never know how much grub you need when on one of these here lake trips, with the chances in favor of something happening to knock the engine out. Besides, remember there will be two more mouths to feed, Thad; and sure I could snatch up some of them fish in a jiffy. Say yes, won't you?"

"No need of it, Giraffe," the other assured the lean scout; "it's true that we'll have a couple more with us, but don't forget that they are expected to have a pretty good supply of food aboard as it is. Then who wants to live on fish diet."

"And we'll get to a place right soon," added Bumpus, "where we can lay in all the stores we want."

"Yes," Step Hen thought fit to remark, "and then too, if we loaded down so with too much fish, what's ever going to become of that game you and

Bumpus are working? We expect to have the table supplied right along now with the product of your combined skills as anglers."

"Oh!" chuckled Giraffe, "after all that honey, I give up, and agree to let things run as they are. But I want to warn the said Bumpus here and now that I'm camping on his trail; and from this time out the fight is agoing to be just fierce!"

"Bah! who's afraid?" sang out the fat scout, with a shrug of his shoulders.

"Everybody get their things together so we can climb aboard as soon as our comrades come close enough to shore. We may have to wade a little, for the landing places are few and far between, and we don't want to take any chances."

"Then I hope some kind friend will have the goodness to carry me on his back; because I sure hate to get my footsies soaked again," remarked Bumpus, unabashed.

It turned out, however, that there was no need of this. The two boys in the motorboat knew how to manage, and brought the little vessel in close enough so that even clumsy Bumpus was able to clamber aboard, after handing up his possessions. And Thad smiled when he saw that the other included among these the rusty crank belonging to the destroyed boat which the poachers had used in their illegal business, evidently romantic Bumpus meant to keep that as a reminder of his little adventure on Sturgeon Island.

Smithy and Bob White were two of the Silver Fox Patrol whom many readers will remember figuring largely in previous books of this series of Boy Scout tales.

They were instantly almost consumed with eagerness to know what had happened to maroon their chums on the island; but until they had passed some distance out Thad would not attempt to relate the stirring circumstances.

"Looky, there they are, ashaking their fists after us; and I reckon they're letting out a few remarks that might burn our ears if we heard the same, which the breeze keeps us from doing," and Giraffe, as he spoke, pointed to where the trio of lawless poachers stood on a rock near the other end of the island.

That was the last they were fated to see of the men. Later on they happened to enter a Canadian port in search of supplies, and of course Thad made it an object to narrate their adventure to some person in authority. The boys heard afterwards that an expedition was at once started out by the Canadian people, looking to the capture of the poacher crowd, and the breaking up of their illegal business; but apparently the other boat must have arrived before them; for while they found the ice pit, just as the boys had described to them, the fish were all gone, nor did a search of the entire island reveal any sign of human occupation.

Of course it did not matter at all to Thad And his chums whether the three men were ever apprehended, as they did not expect to cruise in this region again and consequently there was no chance of their ever meeting any of them afterwards.

They would never be apt to forget the strange things that had come to them however, while marooned on Sturgeon Island; and often when they pored over the Government charts that Thad kept, they could see again in memory many of those adventures looming up along the mental horizon the wreck of the boat; the lively time they had getting ashore; the discovery of the fish packing cabin; the mysterious disappearance of Bumpus; how he was found again under such remarkable conditions; the blowing up of the poachers' boat; and last but not least the opportune arrival of their mates with the other craft.

No doubt many a time the very odor of fish would carry the thoughts of those boys away back to this period in their adventurous careers. Not that it marked the culmination of the good times fortune had in store for them; because before many months passed a splendid chance was going to come along that would give the members of the Silver Fox Patrol an opportunity to enjoy another outing, this time while the North, where their home town lay, was swathed in snow and ice. The title of this next book will be "The Boy Scouts Down in Dixie; or, The Strange Secrets of Alligator Swamp." And the reader of this volume may rest assured that the adventure's befalling Thad and his jolly mates, Allan, Giraffe, Bumpus, Davy, Smithy, Step Hen and the Southern boy, Bob White, will afford them as rich a treat in the new story as anything that has preceded it.

As to that wager between Giraffe and Bumpus, it kept dragging along during the balance of the cruise, sometimes one, and then the other being ahead. But luck finally favored Giraffe, as on the very last day, with the score a tie, he happened to be trailing a stout line out, when his hook became fast to the tail of a big fish that came near pulling him overboard before he succeeded in landing the same, after the engine was hurriedly stopped.

After that Bumpus threw up his hands, and said he would wait on the crowd when they had their dinner upon arriving home; which he certainly did, and with such success that the boys voted he continue to accept "tips" in that vocation whenever they were in camp, Bumpus vigorously dissenting, of course.

Thad learned later an that the poor old Chippeway Belle was fully insured, and no word of complaint ever reached them after they had furnished the owner with all the evidence he needed in order to collect the amount; so there may have been a little truth in what several of the scouts hinted among themselves, that the sinking of the powerboat cleared the air, and allowed the gentleman to replace her with a newer model. "Blessings often come, in disguise," Bumpus says, as he looks up at that rusty crank, tied with a red bow of ribbon, and hanging from the wall of his den at home; and then feeling of his head to ascertain whether that lump has fully subsided, he is apt to go on to remark that sometimes they even drop down from trees, and give a fellow the queerest kind of a thump; for if he had not conceived that little plan of hiding a part of the machinery belonging to the poachers' boat, things might have turned out vastly different from what they did.

The End

Milton Keynes UK
Ingram Content Group UK Ltd.
UKHW010703260923
429409UK00004B/367